Goosebumps®

SON of SLAPPY

R.L. STINE

SCHOLASTIC

Scholastic Children's Books
An imprint of Scholastic Ltd
Euston House, 24 Eversholt Street, London, NW1 1DB, UK
Registered office: Westfield Road, Southam, Warwickshire, CV47 0RA
SCHOLASTIC, GOOSEBUMPS, GOOSEBUMPS HORRORLAND
and associated logos are trademarks and/or registered trademarks of Scholastic
Inc.

First Published in the US by Scholastic Inc, 2013
First published in the UK by Scholastic Ltd, 2017

ISBN 978 1407 17884 4

Goosebumps books created by Parachute Press, Inc.

A CIP catalogue record for this book
is available from the British Library.

Printed by CPI Group (UK) Ltd, Croydon, CR0 4YY
Papers used by Scholastic Children's Books are made
from wood grown in sustainable forests.

3 5 7 9 10 8 6 4 2

www.scholastic.co.uk

WELCOME. YOU ARE MOST WANTED.

Come in. I'm R.L. Stine. Welcome to the Goosebumps office.

Just step around that big hole in the floor. We call that hole The Bottomless Pit. Do you know why?

Because it's a bottomless pit! Ha-ha.

We filled the pit with alligators once. But it didn't work out. The alligators escaped and started swallowing people in the office.

I hate when that happens — don't you?

Yes, that's the laptop I use to write all the Goosebumps books. I know it looks strange. That's because someone's *lap* is still attached.

Don't touch it. I think it's contagious.

I see you are admiring the WANTED posters on the wall. Those posters show the creepiest, crawliest, grossest villains of all time. They are the MOST WANTED bad guys from the MOST WANTED Goosebumps books.

I am telling their stories in the Goosebumps: MOST WANTED series.

Yes, that face with the wide, evil grin and the glassy stare belongs to a ventriloquist dummy. His name is Slappy, and he may be the most ghoulish villain in Goosebumps history.

A boy named Jackson Stander can tell you all about him.

Jackson found himself living a double nightmare with Slappy — *and* the Son of Slappy. To his horror, he quickly learned that two Slappys are NOT better than one!

Go ahead. Read Jackson's story. Better read it with all the lights on and all the doors locked.

You'll quickly find out why Slappy is . . . MOST WANTED.

1

My name is Jackson Stander. I'm twelve, and I know a secret.

You don't have to ask. I'm going to share my secret with you. When I tell you what it is, you might laugh at me.

My sister, Rachel, laughs at me. She rolls her eyes and groans and calls me a goodie-goodie.

But I don't care. Rachel is in trouble all the time, and I'm not. And that's because of my secret, which I'm going to share with you now:

It's a lot easier to be good than to be bad.

That's the whole thing. You're probably shaking your head and saying, "What's the big deal? What kind of crazy secret is that?"

It's simple. Let me explain. I try hard to do the right thing all the time. I try to be nice to everyone, and work hard in school, and be cheerful and kind, and help people when I can, and just be a good dude.

3

This makes Rachel sick. She's always poking her finger down her throat and making gagging sounds whenever I say or do something nice.

Rachel is a real sarcastic kid and a trouble-maker. She likes to argue with her teacher, and she gets into fights with kids in her class. She hates it when the teachers say, "Why can't you be more like your brother, Jackson?"

What does she call me? She calls me *Robot*. She says I'm some kind of goodie-goodie machine.

You've probably guessed that Rachel and I don't get along that well, even though she's just a year younger than me.

We both look a lot alike, too. We're kind of average height. We have straight brown hair and brown eyes, and we both have freckles on our noses and dimples when we smile.

Rachel hates her dimples and her freckles. She says she *hates* it that she looks more like Dad than like Mom. Of course, that doesn't make Dad very happy. He calls Rachel "Problem Child." Mom scolds him every time he says it.

But she *is* a problem child. Mainly, she's *my* problem because she's always in my face. And she's always testing me, teasing me. Trying to make me lose it, blow up, get steamed, start to shout, or fight.

Rachel's mission in life is to get me in trouble with Mom and Dad. She's always trying to make me look bad. But she's so lame. There's *no way* she can win.

A few weeks ago, she was doing an art project in her room and spilled red paint on her floor. She went running to Mom and said, "Jackson was messing around with my paint, and look what he did."

Of course, Mom didn't believe her for a second. Why would I be messing around with *her* paint?

Last night before dinner, Rachel was helping Mom carry the food to the table. She tripped over Sparky, our cat, and dropped a platter of chicken — and it went flying all over the floor.

"Jackson tripped me!" Rachel told Mom.

I was standing all the way across the room. How lame was that?

But Rachel keeps trying.

Now, please don't get me wrong. I'm not perfect. If I told you I'm perfect, that would be obnoxious. Besides, no one is perfect.

I just try to do my best. I really do believe it's easier to be good than bad.

It's something I knew from the time I was a tiny kid.

And then something happened.

Something happened, and I turned bad. I turned very bad. No. Let's tell the truth. I, Jackson Stander, became *evil.*

And that's what this story is all about.

2

We have two canaries at the YC. I gave them their names — Pete and Repete. I can't really tell which one is which, but I pretend.

After school on Wednesday, I was showing a bunch of kids how to pick up the canaries in your hand when you want to clean their cage.

YC stands for Youth Center. Actually, it's called the Morton Applegate Jr. Borderville Youth Center. But no one remembers who Morton Applegate Jr. is. And everyone knows we live in the town of Borderville. So people just call it the YC.

A lot of little kids go to the YC after school. They stay till their parents pick them up after work.

The YC playroom is very bright and cheerful. The walls are shiny red and yellow with funny cows and sheep painted upside down all over them, as if it was raining cows and sheep. The room has shelves to the ceiling, crammed with games and books and art supplies and puzzles and all kinds of great toys for the little kids.

There are stacks of car tires to bounce and climb on. A big flat screen for playing video games. A fish tank, a rabbit cage, and the canary cage. Plenty of cool stuff to keep the kids busy till their parents arrive.

I like to go there after school when I don't have my piano lessons or tennis practice. I go to help out with the little kids. It's fun to play and read with them. The kids are funny, and they treat me like I'm a big deal.

There's a cute, chubby red-haired kid everyone calls Froggy because he's got a funny, scratchy voice. Froggy is my favorite. He's goofy and says the dumbest things to make everyone laugh. If I had a little brother, I'd like him to be Froggy.

Froggy and another favorite of mine — a little blond-haired girl named Nikki — were watching as I reached into the canary cage. Nikki is very shy and quiet, and speaks in a tiny mouse voice. She has a sad face most of the time. But I know how to make her laugh.

"You have to move your hand in very slowly," I told them. "If you move too fast, you'll scare the canary, and he will start fluttering and flapping and cheeping like crazy."

Froggy, Nikki, and a few other kids watched silently as I tugged open the birdcage door. I slowly slid my open hand into the cage and moved it toward Pete.

"Sshhhh," I whispered. "You have to be very

quiet and very careful." The canary stared at me from his wooden perch. The other one, head tilted to one side, watched from the swing.

"If you squeeze it too hard, will he explode?" Froggy asked in a raspy whisper. "I saw that in a cartoon."

"We don't want him to explode," I whispered. "We have to be very gentle."

I opened my hand and prepared to wrap it around the canary. The bird cheeped softly but didn't move. I held my breath and reached forward.

And someone right behind me screamed, "BOO!"

The canary squawked, fluttered out of my grasp — and darted out the open cage door.

My heart skipped a beat. I swung around. I saw my sister, Rachel, standing behind me, a grin on her face. Guess who shouted *Boo*?

The canary flew up to the ceiling.

Kids shouted in surprise. They chased after him.

The frightened canary flew in wild circles, round and round the room. He darted low. "Catch him!" I cried. "Somebody —"

Hands grabbed at the tiny yellow bird. He swooped high again. And then headed toward the far wall. Kids shrieked and ran after him.

"Nooo!" A scream burst from my throat. I could see where he was flying. "Close the window!" I shouted. "Hurry! Close the window!"

"Noooooo!" I cried out again as the frightened little bird darted right to the open window.

Mrs. Lawson, the head YC counselor, made a frantic dash to the window. But she didn't get there in time.

The canary made a soft *clunnnnk* as it flew into the glass pane above the opening. The bird fell back. He caught his balance in midair. Dropped a few feet. And tried a second dive.

But this time, Mrs. Lawson was there. She slid the window shut just as the canary reached it. Once again, the little bird bounced off the glass.

I raised both hands like a catcher's mitt. And caught him on the first bounce. Gently, I wrapped my hands around him.

His heart was beating so hard, the canary buzzed like a bumblebee. He made weak cheeping cries as it struggled to catch his breath.

I carefully set him down on his perch and latched the birdcage shut. I could see the worried faces all around the room. "Pete is okay," I told everyone.

I narrowed my eyes at my sister. Rachel hadn't moved. She stood there like a statue watching the whole chase. As if it wasn't all her fault.

Kids were still running around in circles. Some of them were cheeping and flapping their arms and pretending to be birds.

"Excitement is over," Mrs. Lawson shouted. She tried to wave the kids back to their seats.

I turned to Rachel. "Why did you do that? Why did you yell *boo*?"

She shrugged. "Beats me. Just a joke, I guess."

"Ha-ha. Funny," I said.

She snickered. "You looked so stupid chasing that dumb canary."

"Rachel, the kids would be really upset if the canary flew away," I told her.

She rolled her eyes. "Sor-ry."

I picked up my backpack from against the wall and started to walk her toward the playroom door. "What are you doing here?" I demanded.

"I came to pick you up. Didn't you see Mom's text?"

I pulled my phone out of my jeans pocket. I saw a message from Mom on the screen:

COME HOME. I HAVE NEWS FOR YOU.

"What kind of news?" I said.

10

Rachel shrugged again. "How should I know?"

I waved good-bye to Mrs. Lawson. I led the way out of the YC building. It was a warm spring afternoon. A big orange sun was lowering itself behind the tall trees in the yard across the street.

The YC is three blocks from our house. We started to walk. Rachel kept deliberately bumping me with her backpack. Once, she swung it so hard, she knocked me off the sidewalk. That made her giggle.

"Are you just coming from school?" I asked. "Why are you so late?"

"They kept me after. It wasn't my fault."

"It's never your fault," I said.

She swung her backpack. I dodged away. "Want to make a big deal about it, Robot? Mr. Perfect Robot?" she snapped. "So I got in trouble. Big whoop."

"I wonder what Mom's news is," I murmured.

"Your Martian parents have come to take you home with them," Rachel said.

I laughed. Sometimes she's pretty funny.

"Jackson, can you help me with my math homework tonight?" she asked.

We waited for two kids on bikes to zoom past. Then we crossed the street. A warm breeze made the evergreen trees on the corner quiver and shake.

"I can't," I said. "I'm going over to Stick's after dinner. Help him with a project."

"How can you go to Stick's?" she demanded. "You think Mom and Dad will let you go out on a school night? When are you going to do your homework?"

"I already did it," I said. "I did it all in school before I left."

"AAAAGGGGH." Rachel let out an angry animal growl. She wrapped both hands around my neck and started to strangle me.

"Let go! Hey — let go!"

Laughing, I had to pry her hands off my throat.

She twisted her face angrily. "You're just so totally perfect, aren't you?" She swept her hand over my head and messed up my hair. "Ha. Now you're not so perfect."

A few minutes later, we stepped into the house through the kitchen door. Mom was sitting at the table. She looked up from her recipe notebook. "Why are you so late?"

"Jackson got in trouble in school," Rachel said. "And he had to stay after."

Mom shook her head. "I know you're lying, Rachel. Jackson doesn't get in trouble."

Rachel tossed her backpack against the wall. "I wasn't lying. I was joking."

"Mom, I saw your text," I said. "What's up?"

"Well, I've got big news for you," she replied. "I'm getting rid of you both."

Rachel and I laughed. Mom was joking, of course. We know her sense of humor. She's always trying to catch us off guard.

Mom wanted to be a stand-up comedian after college. She did an act in comedy clubs and nightclubs. It's a mystery to us how she got to be a bank manager. Dad says she's the funniest bank manager in the U.S.

"Don't laugh. I'm serious," Mom said. "I'm getting rid of you both. For spring break. You've been invited to stay with Grandpa Whitman."

Rachel groaned. "Oh, nooo. He's totally creepy. And I hate that scary old house filled with dolls and toys and all his weirdo collections."

"Give him a break," Mom said. "He probably thinks *you're* weird, too."

"Not funny," Rachel said, frowning. "Everything in that house is scary. Did you know he collects poisonous spiders?"

"Only for snacks," Mom joked.

"And what about that frightening caretaker of his — Edgar?" Rachel said. "He creeps around the house in his black suit and hardly ever talks. He looks like he belongs in a horror movie."

Mom snickered. "Have you seen *yourself* before you brush your hair in the morning? Pretty scary."

"Not funny, Mom," Rachel snapped. "I'm serious. I hate that house. Every room has something scary in it." She shuddered.

"I think Grandpa's house is *awesome*," I said. "I love all the weird stuff he collects. Rachel, remember that whole shelf of man-eating plants?"

She shuddered again. "Grandpa wanted me to stick my hand into that plant and see what it would do. How sick is that?"

"He was teasing you," I said.

"No, he wasn't," Rachel insisted.

Mom shook her head. "Rachel, why don't you have a good attitude like your brother?"

"Because I'm a human — not a robot," Rachel replied.

"He's your grandfather, and he loves you two," Mom said. "And I think he's a little lonely in that big, old house with just the caretaker, Edgar, to talk to. You'll have a good time with him. And it's only a week."

"I'm there!" I said. "I'll bet he has some cool new collections."

14

"A whole week?" Rachel cried. "Mom, he has no Wi-Fi. He has no cell phone reception. I'll be cut off from everybody. I'll be cut off from the whole world. How will I talk to my friends?"

"Smoke signals?" Mom said. "Tell you what. I'll ask your dad to buy you a carrier pigeon. It'll carry notes back and forth. It's like an old-fashioned Internet. You'll love it."

"How funny are you?" Rachel said. "Not."

But she could see that we had no choice. Mom had already told Grandpa Whitman that we would be happy to visit him.

And a few days later, Rachel and I were on the bus, taking the long ride to Grandpa Whitman's house way out in the country.

Rachel tapped away on her phone, sending messages to her friends. I had my portable game-player to keep me busy. I carry it wherever I go.

I love to play *Chirping Chickens*. To tell you the truth, I'm *obsessed* with that game. I love making the chickens fly at the giant warthogs. I love the chirping sound they make and the sick *splaaat* when they hit.

I'm up to level twelve. I just love the game. It's one reason I'm never bored. I can play *Chirping Chickens* for hours.

After a while, Rachel lowered her phone to her lap. She turned to me and bumped my arm. I almost dropped my game-player.

"What's wrong?" I asked.

She raised her dark eyes to mine. "Grandpa Whitman's house is scary. Something bad is going to happen," she whispered. "I just know it."

5

Rachel's frightened expression gave me a chill. But I forced a laugh. "Stop being Miss Gloom and Doom. Can't you lighten up?"

"Can't you *shut* up?" She shoved me.

I started to elbow her in the ribs. But I stopped myself just in time. What was the point? She was determined to have a bad time.

As the bus bounced along, I thought about Grandpa Whitman. His house was over two hundred years old. He said he needed a huge old house with lots of rooms because he'd always been a collector.

He started collecting baseball cards when he was our age. Then he collected comic books. Then he moved on to puppets and weird dolls.

His collections got stranger and stranger. Last time Rachel and I visited, he showed us a closet filled with shrunken heads. Shrunken *human* heads.

Seeing those shriveled, pruney heads made Rachel a little sick. She actually turned a pale shade of green. I think she's hated Grandpa Whitman's house ever since. I know she had some bad nightmares after we got home last time.

The bus turned onto the narrow road that led to Grandpa Whitman's house. We drove under tall trees in deep woods. They tilted over the road, making it almost as dark as night.

"You'll be okay," I told her. "Just don't open any closet doors."

"Don't worry. I won't open *any* doors," Rachel said.

"I can't wait to see his new crocodile pond," I said.

Her mouth dropped open.

"Joking," I said.

"Maybe I'll just stay in my room."

"That's dumb," I told her. "You know Mom is probably right. Grandpa Whitman must be lonely all the way out here. We have to cheer him up. Be good company. And maybe we can help him around the house. You know. Do some chores that he can't do."

"Goodie-goodie," Rachel murmured. She stared at her phone and groaned. "No bars. Do you believe it? How can people *live* with no cell phones?"

Before I could answer, the bus squealed to a stop. I glanced out the window. I saw the long gravel driveway that led up to Grandpa Whitman's house. "Here goes," I murmured.

We climbed down from the bus. The driver helped us with our suitcases. I watched the bus rumble away. Then I turned and led the way up the driveway.

Our shoes crunched on the gravel. We brushed past tall grass that had grown over the sides of the drive. The wild grass and weeds stretched up the sloping hill toward the house.

The big house soon came into view. Giant oak trees guarded the front. They cast a shadow over the house, turning it an eerie shade of blue. Cawing crows flew low over the roof, circling the two tall chimneys on each side.

"It . . . it's like a *horror* movie," Rachel stammered. "Like a haunted house in a horror movie."

"Stop scaring yourself," I said. "So there are crows flying around. What's the big deal? At least they're not bats."

"The bats don't come out till night," Rachel said.

My suitcase started to feel heavy. I shifted it to my other hand.

I gazed up at the house. The windows were all dark. The screen door on the front porch tilted off its hinges. Lots of gray shingles were missing on the front wall.

We walked closer. I could see a small vegetable garden at the side of the house. The high weeds in front gave way to a carefully mowed lawn. Tall pink birds — dozens of them — covered the lawn. They didn't move. They were made of plastic and metal.

Grandpa Whitman's collection of lawn flamingos.

He bragged that he had more flamingos than any zoo.

Rachel laughed. "Those birds are so ridiculous. Why on earth does he have so many of them?"

"Because he's a collector," I said.

I started to say something else — but I stopped.

Was that a boy sitting on the edge of the front porch? He sat stiffly. His skinny legs were crossed. He was dressed in red and wore red shoes. His black hair gleamed in the sunlight.

He didn't move as we walked toward him. He just stared at us with a big grin on his face.

"Who is that?" Rachel asked.

We took a few steps closer. I laughed. It wasn't a boy. It was some kind of big doll.

We stepped up to the front porch. "It's a ventriloquist dummy," I said.

"Weird," Rachel murmured, staring down at its grinning face. "Why is it sitting here on the porch?"

"Beats me." I made a fist and tapped the top of its wooden head. "Hey, dummy."

"Owww!" it cried. *"Don't do that!"*

Rachel let out a scream. She grabbed my arm. We both staggered back a step.

"What's your problem?" the dummy rasped in a tinny, high voice. Its lips moved up and down when it spoke. Its eyes slid from side to side.

"It's . . . alive," Rachel whispered. "Jackson, it . . . it's moving by itself."

"No way," I replied.

"Who's the dummy around here?" it demanded.

And then I heard someone laughing. From the house.

I raised my eyes and saw Grandpa Whitman behind the screen door. He stepped out onto the porch, shaking his head. He waved some kind of black box in his hand.

"Hey, I think I fooled you," he called. "Did I? Did I give you a little scare?" He held up the black box. "A remote control. Moves the dummy's mouth and eyes, and makes him speak."

"You didn't fool us," Rachel said. "No way."

He laughed. "Don't lie. I saw the looks on your faces." He patted the dummy's head. "This is Morty. Cute, isn't he?"

"*Don't touch me!*" he made the dummy say.

We all laughed. Then he wrapped Rachel and me in a big bear hug. "It's so good to see you two." He has a deep voice that booms. He never whispers.

Grandpa Whitman is a tall, heavy man with broad shoulders and a big belly. He has a full head of wavy white hair and bright blue eyes. He always wears denim bib overalls a few sizes too big with a red T-shirt underneath.

Rachel backed out of the hug. She motioned to the dummy on the step. "Do you have more surprises like that waiting for us?"

Grandpa Whitman's blue eyes flashed. Before he could answer, another man came out the front door. He was dressed all in black, as usual — a black suit over a black shirt. His pale, bald head caught the fading sunlight. It appeared to glow like a lightbulb.

"Edgar! There you are," Grandpa Whitman said. He turned to us. "You haven't forgotten Edgar, have you?"

"No way," I said. "Hey, Edgar."

He nodded solemnly. His dark eyes studied Rachel and me coldly. "Hello again," he whispered.

Edgar seldom speaks. When he does, it's only in a whisper.

He takes care of the house and Grandpa Whitman. Grandpa told us: "Edgar is a strange man. But once you get to know him . . . he's even stranger!"

One of Grandpa Whitman's jokes. I think Mom got her wacky sense of humor from him.

Edgar carried our suitcases into the house. The sunlight faded. A cool breeze shook the trees.

"I want to show you my newest purchase," Grandpa Whitman said. He motioned us toward the wide garage behind the house. The garage is big enough for at least four cars. But Grandpa Whitman has it filled up with cartons and cartons of his collections.

He disappeared into the garage. Rachel turned to me. "That dummy gave me the creeps," she whispered. "I hate those things. Uh-oh. What's he bringing out?"

It looked like a coiled-up rope. But as he strode closer, I saw the knotted loop at one end.

"It's a noose!" I cried. "Grandpa — what are you going to do with that?"

His eyes narrowed. His expression suddenly turned hard and angry. "You'll see," he said. "You'll see."

Rachel took a step back. Her eyes were on the thick knot of the rope loop.

23

Grandpa Whitman laughed. "Just kidding you." He waved the rope in his hand. "Actually, this is a valuable noose. That's why I bought it for my noose collection."

"A noose collection?" Rachel shook her head in disbelief.

I reached out and squeezed the rope. "Why is it valuable?" I asked.

Grandpa Whitman ran his hands around the loop. "This is the noose that was used to hang Big Barney Brandywine, the outlaw, in Laramie in 1836," he explained. "I've been trying to buy this noose for years."

"Why bother?" Rachel said. "It's gross."

I squeezed it again. "Wow. Can you imagine?" I said. "Someone was actually hanged by this rope."

"Yuck." Rachel made a disgusted face. "That's horrible. Someone swinging from this rope? I don't want to think about it. Take it away."

Grandpa Whitman patted my shoulder. "Jackson gets the idea. This isn't just a piece of rope. It's a piece of American history."

Grandpa Whitman turned and carried the noose back to the garage.

Rachel gave me a hard poke in the ribs. "*Jackson gets the idea . . . Jackson gets the idea . . .*" She mimicked Grandpa Whitman. "Jackson is perfect. Jackson gets the idea."

She tried to poke me again, but I danced away. "Stop it, Rachel."

"That rope was disgusting. But you had to act like you were so interested in it."

"I *was* interested," I insisted.

Grandpa Whitman came bouncing back across the grass. "What are you two talking about?"

"The noose," I said.

He swept a hand through his white hair. "If you think that noose is scary, come with me," he said. He started walking toward the house. "I'm going to show you the most terrifying creature in the whole house."

7

He pulled open the front door and waved us inside. The front hall was almost as big as our whole house. The walls were covered in big paintings of old-fashioned-looking people. An enormous glass chandelier hung on a thick chain from the high ceiling.

I sniffed. "I smell chocolate."

"I think Edgar is baking a cake," Grandpa Whitman said. "To welcome you."

I peeked into the dark living room. Small purple creatures floated up and down in a tall glass tank.

"Those are my jellyfish," Grandpa Whitman said. "You can check them out later."

"Are they poisonous?" Rachel asked.

"Probably," Grandpa Whitman answered. "Follow me."

He walked to the wide wooden staircase at the side of the room. The carpet on the stairway was tattered and worn. The stairs creaked and groaned as Grandpa Whitman led us up to the second floor.

We followed him down the long, dimly lit hall. We passed a room filled with old radios. Another room had trains set up in a miniature town.

We stopped at the end of the hall. Grandpa Whitman pushed open a door. "Go ahead. Take a look," he said.

Rachel and I stepped into the doorway and peered into the room.

Grandpa Whitman flashed on the light — and we both gasped.

Dozens of ugly, grinning faces stared back at us.

"Oh, wow," I murmured. "I can't believe this. So many dummies!"

The room was jammed with ventriloquist dummies.

I glanced around at half a dozen old-fashioned couches and chairs. Two low coffee tables sat side by side. And there were grinning dummies sprawled over every piece of furniture.

Some sat in little chairs. Several were on the floor with their backs against the wall. I saw a pile of dummies near the window, just heaped on top of one another.

Rachel shook her head. "I hate the way they're all grinning." She turned to Grandpa Whitman. "They're so ugly and creepy. Why do you like them?"

He walked into the room. He smiled at the crowd of dummies. "These are my children."

Rachel rolled her eyes.

"I think I have every famous dummy in history," Grandpa said. "Look. That's Mr. Tipply over there." He pointed to a dummy wearing a black tuxedo and a tall black top hat. "He was in a dozen movies."

He stepped into the middle of the wooden dolls. "That's Charlie Harley and Foo-Foo. And the one with the goofy face and all the freckles? That's Ronnie Rascal."

"Thrills," Rachel whispered.

"They're awesome!" I said. "They are totally cool. They're all different, and they're all so funny looking."

"These are all TV and movie stars," Grandpa Whitman said. "They're all famous."

"Know what?" I told him. "I'd love to have a ventriloquist dummy to entertain the kids at the YC. I could put on great shows. You know. Do a comedy act."

Grandpa scratched the back of his head. "Your mother always wanted to be a comedian. Beats me how she ever became a banker. What a mystery."

I gazed from dummy to dummy. "The kids at the YC would love a funny ventriloquist act," I said.

"They'd love it like a toothache," Rachel muttered.

Grandpa Whitman laughed. "Rachel, you're funny."

"I was *serious*," Rachel insisted.

A dummy in a gray suit and shiny black shoes caught my eye. It was perched in an armchair against the wall, away from the others. Something about this dummy sent a shiver down my back.

Its big head had an evil, red-lipped grin. And it appeared to be smiling right at me. The dummy's dark, painted eyes locked on my face.

"What's that one called?" I asked, pointing.

"That dummy is named Slappy," Grandpa Whitman answered. "Let me tell you about that guy. He's an interesting story."

But before he could begin, Edgar slid into the room. He stepped in front of Rachel and me. His dark eyes were circles of fright.

"Stay away from Slappy," Edgar rasped. *"Stay away from that one. I'm WARNING you!"*

8

Grandpa Whitman's face turned red. "Edgar, don't scare them," he said. "You've got to calm down. You're acting like a frightened child. This dummy has a bad history. But he's totally safe."

Edgar backed away. But his worried expression didn't change. "Listen to me," he whispered. "Stay away from that one."

Grandpa Whitman bumped past him and lifted the dummy from its armchair. "Say hi, Slappy." He made the dummy wave its wooden hand.

"Gross," Rachel muttered.

Grandpa Whitman carried the dummy over to us. "I'll tell you the old legend about him. The legend that has Edgar so worked up."

"It isn't a legend," Edgar insisted. "It's the truth."

Grandpa Whitman laughed. He winked at Rachel and me. "You can believe it if you want to. The story goes that an evil sorcerer carved

Slappy out of coffin wood. And he put a curse on the dummy."

I stared at the dummy's frozen, red-lipped grin. "A curse?"

Grandpa Whitman nodded. "If a bunch of strange words are said aloud, the dummy will come to life. It will turn its owner into a slave. And it will work to spread its evil everywhere."

He made Slappy's mouth open and close. Then Grandpa tilted the head back and made a shrill laughing sound through his teeth. "Anyone who owns Slappy will face a *horrifying* fate," he said.

"It's true. It's true," Edgar whispered. He had backed up to the wall. I saw beads of sweat on his bald head.

Rachel squeezed the dummy's black shoe. Then she raised her eyes to Grandpa Whitman. "What if it *is* true? Why did you buy this dummy? Why did you buy something that could come to life and do horrible things?"

Grandpa shifted the dummy in his arms. "Because this *isn't* Slappy," he said softly.

"Not Slappy? What do you mean?" I asked.

"The original Slappy was destroyed a long time ago," he answered. "He was destroyed so that his evil would die with him. This is only a copy. I call him *Son of Slappy*. This dummy is perfectly harmless."

Rachel frowned at the dummy. "Are you sure?"

Grandpa Whitman nodded. "Only a copy."

"Can I hold him?" I asked.

He settled the dummy into my arms. It was heavier than I thought. The wooden head must have weighed ten pounds!

I made the dummy sit up straight. I reached my hand into its back and fumbled for the controls to make the mouth move up and down.

And suddenly, the dummy screamed in a high, shrill voice: *"Let GO of me! Let GO or I'll punch your teeth out!"*

Rachel opened her mouth in a cry of surprise. "Grandpa — you made the dummy say that, right?"

He shook his head. "No. No, I didn't, Rachel." He raised his right hand. "I swear."

It was my turn to laugh. "I made the dummy say that," I told them. "I guess I'm a pretty good ventriloquist. I totally fooled you both."

Edgar had been silent the whole while. Suddenly, he stepped forward and took the Slappy dummy from my arms.

"This dummy is evil," he said in his throaty whisper. He waved his pale hand around the room. "They're *all* evil. Stay away. Stay out of this room."

Edgar was breathing noisily by the time he finished his warning. Under his black suit jacket, his chest heaved up and down.

Grandpa patted his shoulder, trying to calm him down. "Edgar has some strange ideas,"

Grandpa Whitman said. "He frightens easily." He turned his gaze on Rachel and me. "But *you* don't — *do* you?"

The days went quickly for me, slowly for Rachel. She wasn't even trying to have a good time. And she kept getting in my face for being so cheerful.

"Don't you miss talking to your friends?" she demanded. She shook her phone. "It's useless here. Totally useless. My friends have probably all forgotten me by now."

"Rachel, it's only been four days," I said.

I kept busy the whole time. I played *Chirping Chickens* a lot. I got up to level fifteen.

I helped Grandpa Whitman weed his garden. And I helped to build some new shelves for his model car collection.

One afternoon, I found an amazing collection of old board games. I dragged some to the dining room table and begged my sister to play them with me.

"No way," she said. "Look at them. They've turned moldy green. And they smell horrible. They're *putrid*."

Grandpa Whitman showed her his incredible collection of antique dolls. Some of them were over two hundred years old. "Too smelly," Rachel declared, holding her nose.

Grandpa laughed. But I could see he was upset.

"You're hurting his feelings," I said after he left the room.

Rachel shrugged. "I have to be honest — don't I?"

Soon, it was time to leave. Edgar carried out our suitcases and slid them into the back of Grandpa Whitman's old van.

We said good-bye to Grandpa on the front porch. A breeze fluttered his white hair. His blue eyes seemed faded. He suddenly looked older. I guess he really was sorry to see us leave.

He hugged Rachel. "I hope you weren't too bored."

"Bored? This place is too crazy to get bored in."

That made Grandpa Whitman laugh.

Then it was my turn for a good-bye hug. "I had an awesome time," I told him. "I loved the old board games and the weird magazines and the old model cars. But I think Son of Slappy was my favorite. I can't wait to tell the kids at the YC about him and all your ventriloquist dolls."

"Maybe you two can visit me again before school starts in the fall," Grandpa Whitman said. "I promise I won't scare you — too much." He chuckled.

More hugs. Then we waved good-bye and followed Edgar to the van. It was a short drive to the bus station. Edgar didn't say a word. He had a news station on the radio. He listened to it and kept his eyes straight ahead on the road.

A few minutes later, the van rumbled up to the little bus station. Rachel and I slid out of the van.

Edgar pulled our suitcases from the back and set them down on the pavement. He wiped sweat off his bald head.

"Bye, Edgar," I said. "Thanks for driving us."

He didn't answer. His eyes went wide and he leaned closer. "*I warned you,*" he rasped. "*I warned you. Be careful. You asked for it.*"

10

Mom and Dad picked us up at the bus station. They carried on as if we'd been gone for months. "Did you have a great time?" Dad asked.

"It was awesome," I said.

"Great," Rachel mumbled. She sat beside me in the backseat of the car with her phone in her hands, frantically texting her friends.

"Did your grandfather try to scare you?" Mom asked.

"Every chance he had," I replied.

Mom laughed. "My dad is so crazy. When I was a little girl, I lived in terror. I jumped at every sound. He loved to make me scream."

"Well, he's still doing it," Rachel muttered, eyes on her phone. "Horrible."

"No. It was kind of fun," Mom said. "After a while, I started scaring him back. Once, I even put a tarantula in his bed. Under the covers. Believe that?"

"What happened?" I asked.

37

"It bit him in the butt. He didn't think it was funny."

"Ooh, Mom got into trouble," Rachel said. "I guess I take after you, Mom."

"I don't know *who* you take after," Mom joked. "Godzilla, maybe."

"Oh, thanks a bunch!" Rachel exclaimed. Her thumbs tapped away on her phone.

Back in my room, I hoisted the suitcase to my bed. I clicked it open and pulled up the lid.

A grinning face gazed up at me.

"Huh?" I uttered a startled cry. "Son of Slappy?"

I stared down at the dummy. Its arms and legs were carefully folded under my clothes.

How did it get in my suitcase?

I suddenly realized that Rachel was standing beside me. "I don't believe it!" she cried. "You wanted that dummy so badly, you STOLE it!"

"N-no —" I stammered.

"Yes!" she said. "You said you wanted it — and you *took* it!"

"No. No way!" I said. "Listen — I'll bet Edgar put it in there. He was so eager to get it out of the house."

"Liar!" Rachel cried. "Liar! You *stole* it!"

She spun away from me and ran out into the hall. "Mom! Dad!" she screamed. "Jackson stole something from Grandpa Whitman! Come up here! Goodie-goodie Jackson stole something!"

I heard my parents stampeding up the stairs. They burst into my room with confused looks on their faces. "What's up? What's all the shouting?" Dad demanded.

Rachel pulled the dummy from my suitcase and held it up to them. "Look. Jackson isn't as perfect as you think. He stole this. He stole this dummy from Grandpa Whitman."

Dad squinted hard at me. Mom gasped. "That's horrible, Jackson. How could you steal from your own grandfather?"

"I — I — I —" I stammered. "No way —"

"We can't put up with a thief in this house," Dad said, shaking his head. "Jackson, I'm totally disappointed with you."

"But —"

I stared hard at the grinning dummy. Was Edgar right about it? Was it truly evil?

The dummy had already gotten me into major trouble.

Was this only the beginning?

11

Rachel had a sick grin on her face. She was enjoying this moment a lot. She loved seeing *me* in trouble instead of her.

"I . . . I didn't steal the dummy," I stammered. "I opened my suitcase and —"

Mom and Dad burst out laughing.

"Jackson, don't look so serious," Mom said. "Couldn't you tell we were teasing you?"

Dad turned to Rachel. "What's wrong with you, Rachel? We all know Jackson would never do anything like that."

Mom shook her head. Her green eyes flashed. "The idea of Jackson stealing something . . . That's just silly."

Rachel shoved the dummy into my arms. Its big wooden head bumped my nose hard. "Ouch!" Pain shot over my face.

Rachel laughed.

Rubbing my nose, I lowered the Son of Slappy to the bed. "I told Grandpa Whitman I'd love to have a dummy to entertain the kids at the YC," I told my parents. "I guess he decided to give me this one."

"Let's call to make sure," Mom said.

I found my cell phone on the dresser. I pushed Grandpa Whitman's number. The phone rang and rang.

"No answer," I said. "And he doesn't have voice mail."

Mom sighed. "My dad *never* answers the phone. Would it kill him to pick up?"

Dad patted Mom on the shoulder. "He's probably off somewhere dealing with one collection or another. Nowhere near the phone."

I clicked the phone off. Dad went back downstairs.

"I'll help you unpack," Mom said. She started pulling dirty clothes from my suitcase.

Rachel plopped down on my bed. She took the dummy's hand and pretended to pick his nose with it. She's a riot, isn't she?

"Hey, didn't you notice the box on your bed?" Mom asked.

I turned and saw a flat, rectangular box wrapped with blue-and-red glittery paper. I reached for it. "What's this?"

"It's an early birthday present," Mom said. "From your aunt Ada. Go ahead. Open it."

Rachel grabbed it out of my hands. "Let *me* open it." She ripped at the wrapping paper and tossed hunks of it onto the floor. Then she yanked open the box and pulled out a gray-and-black sweater.

I felt the sleeve. Very soft. "Cool," I said. "That's awesome."

Rachel tossed the sweater onto the bed. "What about me?" she demanded. "Why don't I get a present? It's *my* birthday soon."

"Don't be upset," Mom told her. "Aunt Ada said your present is coming later."

Rachel made a face. "How come Jackson always comes first?"

"Don't be a baby," Mom said quietly. She pulled a pair of balled-up socks from the suitcase and closed the suitcase lid.

Rachel climbed down from my bed. "Hey, I just remembered, Mom. I have a present for you and Dad."

She disappeared into her room and returned a few seconds later carrying a big glass jar. She pushed it into Mom's hands. "It's honey," she said.

Mom studied it. "Honey? Where from?"

"From Grandpa's new beehive." Rachel said. "He gave it to me to take home."

"Nice," Mom said. She flashed Rachel a smile. "I'll put it down in the pantry. We can all enjoy it on pancakes tomorrow morning."

"I don't want Jackson to have any," Rachel said.

Mom squinted at her. "Why not?"

"Because he got a sweater and I didn't."

"You're ridiculous," Mom said. She put two hands on Rachel's shoulders and guided her out of my room.

As soon as they were gone, I picked up the dummy and sat it on my lap. I fumbled under its gray suit jacket to find the controls in back for its mouth and eyes.

A small square of white paper fell out of the suit pocket. *Maybe it's a note from Grandpa Whitman,* I thought.

I picked it up and unfolded it. No. Not a note from my grandfather.

My eyes moved over the strange words printed on the page:

KARRU MARRI ODONNA LOMA MOLONU KARRANO.

I moved my lips, saying them silently to myself. I realized these must be the words that brought the original Slappy to life.

The sheet of paper trembled in my hand.

Should I read the words out loud?

12

I gazed at the dummy's grinning face. The lips were painted a glossy red. One nostril had a tiny chip in the wood. The glassy eyes stared blankly back at me. I rubbed one hand over the wavy wooden hair.

This isn't the real Slappy, I told myself. *The original Slappy was evil, according to Grandpa Whitman. This dummy is just a copy.*

So if I read the strange words . . . nothing will happen.

I pulled the sheet of paper closer to my face and started to read: *"Karru Marri . . ."*

No.

I stopped. I felt a chill run down my back.

Why look for trouble?

I tucked the paper into the dummy's jacket pocket. I set him down in a corner and changed into my pajamas for bed.

* * *

44

The next morning, a Saturday, we had pancakes and honey for breakfast.

Sweet. Rachel complained that I was using too much of her honey. But she's crazy. The jar was still almost full.

After breakfast, I went up to my room to practice with Slappy. I wanted to figure out how to work his eyes and mouth. And I wanted to think up some jokes to tell with him. Stuff the kids at the YC would like.

I sat on the edge of the bed and put the dummy on my lap. I found the eye control in his back and made his eyes slide from side to side. Then I made his mouth open and close. He was pretty easy to control.

"How are you today, Slappy?" I said.

I kept my teeth together and made him reply. *"I feel as good as I look — fabulous!"*

"Tell me, why do they call you Slappy?"

"Raise my hand to your face and I'll show you!"

Hey, pretty good. I was pretty good at talking without moving my lips.

The piece of paper in the jacket pocket caught my eye. I pulled it out and read the words silently to myself once again.

It was tempting. Really. Tempting to read the words out loud. Especially since this dude was just a copy of Slappy.

45

But I kept picturing Edgar's frightened face. And I kept remembering his warning to keep away from the dummy.

I was still holding the piece of paper when I heard the thunder of footsteps on the stairs. A few seconds later, my two best friends — Mickey and Miles — burst into my room.

Mickey Haggerty is tall and as thin as a broomstick. His nickname is actually Stick. He has long coppery hair and strange green eyes that look like cat eyes. And I've never seen him when he wasn't grinning.

Miles Naylor is African American, shorter than Stick and me. But he works out and looks a lot more athletic than the two of us. He has very short hair, just like a layer of fuzz over his head, dark brown eyes that make him look more serious than he is, and a deep voice.

Miles's voice changed before anyone else's in our class. He says it's because he's more mature than everyone else. But that doesn't compute. He's as big a goof as anyone in the class.

They both started to laugh when they saw me sitting on the bed with the dummy in my lap.

"You're playing with baby dolls?" Miles said.

"Ha-ha. No. Look," Stick said. "He has the doll on his lap. He's practicing for when he has a girlfriend."

They both thought that was a riot. They bumped knuckles and hee-hawed.

"It's not a doll," I said. "It's a ventriloquist dummy."

They squinted at it. "Can you make him talk?" Stick asked.

"Which one is the dummy?" Miles asked.

More laughter.

"His name is Slappy," I said. "I'm going to do a comedy act with him."

"But you're not funny, Jackson," Stick said. "You're about as funny as stomach flu."

"No way," Miles chimed in. "He's not that funny."

"Give me a break," I groaned. "I'm going to think up some jokes. You know. It's for the kids at the YC after school."

"Yeah, sure." Miles rolled his eyes. "You can admit it, dude. We're your friends. You just like to play with dolls."

"Maybe you and the doll should have a tea party," Stick joked.

"Not funny," I said. "You guys are starting to steam me. Look at this dummy's face. Does he look like a cute doll to you?"

I turned Slappy's head so he was gazing at them.

That shut them both up.

"He looks evil, right?" I said. "Well, guess what. He *is* evil."

I was so tired of being teased, I decided to give my two friends a good scare. I told them the

47

story of Slappy that Grandpa Whitman told Rachel and me. I told them how he had evil powers and how he could be brought to life by reading a bunch of strange words.

And then I held up the page of strange words. "Should I read them?" I asked.

I didn't tell them this wasn't the real Slappy. I didn't tell them this was just a copy. I really wanted to scare them.

But guess what? They both laughed.

Stick shook his head. "You really believe that story, Jackson?"

"I've seen it in some creepy movies," Miles said. "But *no way* a stupid wooden dummy can come to life."

"Okay. You asked for it," I said.

I sat Slappy up in my lap. And I raised the words close to my face. "*Karru . . . Marri . . . Odonna . . .*"

"Whoa. Wait a minute." Miles grabbed my arm. His expression had changed. He looked a little frightened. "When your grandfather told you that story about the dummy, do you think he was just trying to scare you?"

"No," I said. "Grandpa Whitman believed it. He swore it was true."

Stick and Miles studied the dummy silently. They had stopped laughing and joking.

"He said the dummy has incredible evil," I said.

My two friends exchanged glances. "Well . . . maybe you shouldn't read the words," Stick said.

"Just in case," Miles said. "Maybe you'd better skip it."

"Well . . . okay," I replied. I started to set the piece of paper down.

But before I could move, Rachel came running into the room. I knew she'd been outside the door the whole time. She loved spying on me, hoping to get me in some kind of trouble.

She raced across the room, grabbed Slappy into her arms, and swiped the paper from my hand.

"Hey — give that back!" I cried. I jumped up from the bed and grabbed for it, but she swung it out of my reach.

And then she shouted the words at the top of her lungs: "*Karru Marri Odonna Loma Molonu Karrano!*"

Rachel tossed back her head and laughed.

Stick and Miles stood frozen in front of the bed, watching Rachel and the dummy in silence.

"Rachel — I told you to stay out of my room," I said. "You're not funny. Give me that dummy."

I reached out both hands for it. But I stopped when the dummy MOVED.

Slowly, it raised its head. It gazed at my friends. Then it turned to me. *And it winked one eye.*

"Oh, no. Oh, no," I moaned. "Rachel — what have you *done*?"

13

The dummy's head slumped down. Rachel squinted at me. "Jackson, what's your problem?"

"It — it moved," I stammered. "You said those words, and the dummy started to move."

"Are you totally losing it?" Rachel said. "It did not."

I turned to my friends. "You saw it, right? You saw the dummy sit up and wink at me?"

They both shook their heads. Stick snickered. "You're nuts, Jackson."

"He's trying to scare us," Miles said. "Oooh, I'm scared. I'm scared."

They both collapsed on my bed, hee-hawing.

I stared at the dummy. It was slumped life-lessly on its back in Rachel's arms. *Did I imagine that it moved?*

Of course I did. I imagined the whole thing. I reminded myself that this dummy was just a copy.

She pushed the dummy into my hands. "Take it. It's dumb. And it's almost as ugly as you are."

"Whoa. Little sister disses Jackson!" Miles exclaimed. "Nasty."

Rachel hurried out of the room. I took the dummy and propped it against the wall.

"I have to tell you the truth," I told my two friends. "This isn't the real Slappy. It's only a copy. My grandfather gave it to me. He called it the Son of Slappy."

Stick grinned at me. "So this one can't come to life?"

"No. This one can't come to life," I said. "It's not the evil dummy from the legend. I was just trying to scare you. But for a moment, I scared *myself*!"

I glanced at the clock on my wall. "Oh, wow. I'm late," I said. "I promised I'd go to the YC and help out with the kids this morning. Got to go, guys."

Miles jumped to his feet. Stick patted the dummy on its head. "Hey, Slappy," he said. "Don't scare Jackson too badly."

Miles laughed. "Yeah. Jackson's scared of dolls."

I rolled my eyes. "You guys are a total riot. Remind me to laugh sometime."

They both started to the door. "Later," they said in unison.

"Later," I repeated.

They disappeared down the stairs.

I changed my shirt and pulled on a pair of sneakers. I tucked my game-player into my jeans pocket. Sometimes the kids liked to play *Chirping Chickens* with me.

At the door, I turned back to Slappy.

Should I bring him and show him off to the kids?

No, I decided. *I'll wait till I have a totally awesome comedy act with him. Then I can show him off.*

I clicked off the light and started to leave. And Slappy tumbled onto his stomach.

"Huh?" I gasped.

Did he move? Again?

No. No way. He just fell over. That's all.

I closed the door behind me and headed down the stairs.

14

I found about a dozen kids in the playroom at the YC. A bunch of them were climbing around on the tires. Some were just chasing each other in a wild race around the room. My little friend Froggy sat in a corner looking at a picture book.

The canaries were chirping their yellow heads off. "I think they're hungry," I said. "Does anyone want to help me feed them?"

A bunch of kids came running. Froggy set down his book and came over, too.

I pulled the bag of birdseed from the supply closet and carried it over to the cage. I showed the kids how to slide the plastic bird feeder off the cage. I started to fill it when I heard a voice behind me.

I turned and saw Mrs. Pearson in the doorway. I was surprised to see her. Mrs. Pearson is the director of the YC. But she hardly ever comes in on Saturdays.

She's a tall, thin woman with black hair streaked with gray. She's older than my parents. But she always dresses in jeans and brightly colored T-shirts.

She is usually smiling but not today. She gazed around the roomful of kids, biting her bottom lip, a frown on her face.

She walked over to Mrs. Lawson's desk and said a few words to her. I couldn't hear what they were saying. Mrs. Lawson kept shaking her head.

I filled the seed cup and let Froggy place it back in the cage. The two canaries dove for it. I guess they really *were* hungry.

I turned away from the cage when Mrs. Pearson called to me. "Jackson, can I speak to you for a minute?"

I followed her out into the hall. *Am I in trouble?* The thought flashed into my mind. *Is she angry about the canary getting loose?*

My heart started to pound a little faster.

The hall was empty. The bright yellow walls gleamed under the ceiling lights. A sign on the wall said: ONLY 2 DAYS TO SIGN UP FOR THE TENNIS TOURNAMENT.

Someone left the *r* out of tournament. I'm a very good speller. I always catch mistakes like that. One of the things Rachel hates about me. She can't spell her own name! Ha-ha.

We stopped in front of Mrs. Pearson's office door. I leaned a shoulder against the wall. She flashed me a quick smile, but her eyes didn't look happy.

"Jackson, it's so nice of you to come in and help out on Saturdays," she said.

"Uh . . . thank you," I replied. "I . . . like it."

"Well, most boys wouldn't want to give up their Saturdays to help a bunch of little kids. But you're so good with them. You're so kind and patient. And the kids really like you."

I could feel my face growing hot. Why do I always blush when someone compliments me?

"Thank you," I said. I couldn't think of anything else to say.

"I'm afraid I have bad news," she said. She bit her bottom lip again. "The YC is in real trouble. We are running out of money. And the town has no money to give us. I'm afraid we may have to shut down."

"That's terrible," I said. I heard kids laughing down the hall in the playroom. "That's so sad. Those kids love it here."

She nodded. "We are going to try to keep it going. To raise some money. We are planning a huge bake sale and a stage show in the auditorium. If we work hard, we can raise enough money to keep the YC going for another year."

I stared at her. Down the hall, the kids burst into laughter again.

"Jackson, I hope you will help us with our bake sale and stage show," Mrs. Pearson said.

"Perhaps you could write a skit for the kids to perform?"

"No problem," I said. "That would be fun."

"And maybe you could do some kind of act yourself," she said. "Do you have any ideas?"

I laughed. "I just got a ventriloquist dummy," I told her. "I was planning to work up a comedy act with it. You know. For the kids."

"Perfect!" Mrs. Pearson gushed. "The audience will love that, Jackson."

Her expression turned serious. She put a hand on my shoulder. "I'm counting on you," she said. "I know we can save the YC — with your help."

"Yes," I said. "No problem."

Three words. Three little words.

How could I know that those three words would lead to unbelievable horror?

How could I know that those three words would lead to the worst day of my life?

15

"Nice throw, ace!" Stick shouted.

The Nerf football bounced over the hedge into the neighbor's yard. "Guess I don't know my own strength," I said.

I took a running start and tumblesaulted over the hedge. Wolfie, Stick's big German shepherd, started to bark ferociously. "He's just jealous," I said, "because he can't do that."

I grabbed the blue rubber football and tossed it back to Stick. Then I pushed myself through the hedge back into his yard.

I saw Miles trotting up the asphalt driveway. His open red shirt was flapping in the wind as he ran. His white sneakers reminded me of big marshmallows, padding on the drive. "Hey, what's up?" he called.

Stick heaved him the football. It sailed through Miles's hands and bounced off the garage wall. "Nice catch!" Stick yelled.

Miles picked the ball up and heaved it with all his strength at Stick's stomach. Stick let out a cry and spun away, and the ball bounced off his shoulder.

A typical ball game for the three of us. It always starts out like a nice game of toss and catch. And then all of a sudden, we're pounding each other black-and-blue with the ball.

It was a warm, sunny Sunday afternoon. It had rained the night before, and the grass sparkled from the raindrops. Not a cloud in the sky. I kept raising my face to the sun. The sunlight felt so warm and soft.

The three of us were meeting in Stick's backyard to talk about the YC bake sale. All the schools in Borderville were competing to bake the best dessert — and raise the most money for the YC.

I tossed the football to Miles. "What should we make?" I asked. "It has to be something awesome. You know. Something that will *crush* the other schools."

Miles sent the ball sailing over Stick's head. Stick chased after it, but Wolfie got there first. The big dog snapped the ball up in his teeth and ran off with it. We watched him gallop away around the side of the house.

"Hey — what's up with that?" Miles said.

"Wolfie's not a team player," Stick said.

"We've got to concentrate," I said. "What can we bake?"

"How about apple pie?" Miles said. "Everyone loves apple pie."

"What's special about that?" I asked.

He shrugged. "Well . . . we could pile on a gallon or two of ice cream."

"That's not special," Stick said. He bumped Miles hard with his shoulder. The two of them began wrestling on the grass.

I crossed my arms in front of me and waited for them to stop. But they kept rolling around, elbowing each other, grunting and growling. They stopped when they smashed into Wolfie's enormous bathtub.

"Ow!" Miles cried out as he banged his head on the big metal tub.

Stick laughed. "Did your head dent the tub?"

Miles climbed to his feet, groaning and rubbing his head.

"You just gave me an idea," I said. I crossed the yard and picked up the big, round tub in both hands.

"You want to give my dog a bath?" Stick said.

"Shut up," I said. "Listen to me. This is *genius*."

"And he's so modest," Miles said. He helped pull Stick up off the grass.

"We use this tub," I said. "We fill it with cake batter."

"Genius!" Stick cried. He slapped me on the back.

"Let me finish," I said. "We fill the tub with chocolate cake batter. And we make the biggest chocolate cupcake ever made. Tell the truth. Genius?"

They stared at the tub. I could see they were thinking hard about it.

"We'll need a lot of icing," Miles said.

Stick nodded. "How much cake batter will we need?" He took the tub from me and studied the outside of it. "It says here it's a ten-gallon tub."

"So we'll need ten gallons of cake batter?" Miles said.

"Maybe," I said. "Wouldn't that be awesome?"

"We could get our cupcake in the Guinness Book of Records," Stick said. "I was reading that book. It's got the biggest pizza in the world and the person with the longest beard. Stuff like that. We could be in it with the biggest cupcake ever."

"Let's ask your mom if she has any cake batter recipes," I said. "Maybe she can help us figure out how much batter we need to put in the tub."

We tromped into the house and found Mrs. Haggerty reading a book in the den. She's very tall and pretty, and has blond hair piled high on her head. Stick doesn't look anything like her. She always says she found him under a tree.

60

Mrs. Haggerty isn't a stand-up comic like my mom was. But she's really funny.

"Hey, guys," she said. "Are you two staying for dinner? Stick's dad is bringing home a couple of pizzas."

"I can't," I said. "I told my mom I'd be home. But . . . we wanted to ask you a question."

She closed her book. "What's up?"

"We want to use Wolfie's dog tub and make the world's biggest cupcake," Stick said. "You know. For the YC bake sale."

"It's a big contest," Miles added. "Every school in town is competing."

"But the world's biggest cupcake would definitely win," Stick said.

"Definitely," his mom said. "And how can I help you?"

"We need to know how much cake batter to make to go in the tub," Stick said.

Mrs. Haggerty blinked. Then she started to laugh.

The three of us just stared at her. We waited for her to stop.

"I'm sorry," she said finally. "I'm sorry, but it's funny. There's one thing you boys didn't think of."

"What?" Stick demanded.

"After you fill the tub with cake batter, how will you bake it? It won't fit in any oven."

My mouth dropped open. Stick shut his eyes.

61

Miles let out a groan. He slapped his forehead. "Stupid, stupid."

"It seemed like a good idea," I said.

"It was a stupid idea," Miles said.

"Sometimes stupid ideas are good," Mrs. Haggerty said. "Stupid ideas can spark your imagination and lead to good ideas."

"My imagination isn't sparked," Stick said. "I could just picture that giant cupcake."

I glanced at the clock on the bookshelf. I was late for Sunday dinner. "Let's keep thinking," I said. "I'm sure we can think up a lot more stupid ideas."

I meant it as a joke, but no one laughed. I said good-bye and trotted the two blocks to my house.

My problems didn't start until after dinner.

As I climbed the stairs to my room, I was still thinking about the huge cupcake. There *must* be some way to bake ten gallons of cake batter.

I stepped into my room and clicked on the light. The first thing I saw was the Slappy dummy sitting up straight on my bed, his back against the wall.

Weird, I thought. *Didn't I leave him on the floor?*

I guessed Rachel had been playing with him.

I sat down on the bed and reached for him.

And to my horror, *he reached for ME!*

His arms shot up. I uttered a gasp as his wooden hands grabbed me by the throat.

16

"You — you —" I choked out. "You're really ALIVE!"

The wooden fingers tightened around my neck. I struggled to breathe. My heart pounded so hard, my chest ached.

This can't be happening.

I tried to jerk free. But I couldn't break away. Pain rocketed up and down my body.

The dummy lowered his big head toward me. His mouth clicked up and down. "Please thank Rachel for bringing me to life."

His voice was high and shrill. I thought of chalk squeaking on a chalkboard.

His glassy eyes bulged wide. "Now the fun begins!" he shouted in my ear.

"L-let go," I stammered. The hard wooden fingers gripped my throat, squeezing tight.

He tossed back his head and cackled, an ugly, frightening laugh. "I won't let go! You can't make me!"

63

"But . . . but . . ." I sputtered. "You're a copy. You're not the real Slappy."

He cackled again. "Who would believe that lie? Only a dumb sap like your grandfather!"

I grabbed his wrists and struggled to pull his hands off me. As we wrestled, the truth repeated in my head. This was the *real* Slappy, in all his evil. And my sister had shouted out the words to bring him to life.

"Ahhh!" With a hoarse cry, I tugged his hands off my throat. I slapped them down and leaped to my feet. My whole body trembled as I spun around to face him.

"You're Slappy. You're the original Slappy," I said.

The wooden face grinned up at me with its painted red lips. The mouth clicked as it talked.

"Yes, that's me, Jackson, my friend. I'm the one and only. But don't feel bad. Your grandfather didn't lie. There *is* a Son of Slappy."

I gazed down at this horrible-looking thing, this wooden puppet, who could speak and move and grinned with such evil.

"Jackson," it rasped, "don't you want to know who the Son of Slappy is? Aren't you curious?"

His round black eyes locked on mine. And I suddenly felt strange. Suddenly weak. My mind . . . I couldn't think of words. I couldn't speak.

I could feel the dummy invading my mind. It was like he was hypnotizing me. Seeping into my brain . . . my thoughts.

And I couldn't do anything to keep him out.

I felt as if I was swimming underwater. I suddenly felt as if I was sinking . . . sinking into a deep darkness.

I struggled to speak. Finally, I shouted: "Who? Tell me. Who is the Son of Slappy?"

"YOU!" the dummy shrieked. It bounced up and down with excitement.

"Huh?"

"Congratulations, Jackson. It's you, you lucky boy. YOU are now the Son of Slappy!"

I heard a sound. A loud *chirp*.

Suddenly, I felt dizzy. The room began to spin. My head felt heavy.

Once again, the dummy tossed back its head and opened its mouth wide in an ugly, shrill laugh.

And to my horror, I couldn't stop myself.

My head tilted back — just like his — and I laughed right along with him.

17

The next thing I knew, I was under the covers in my bed. I blinked myself awake. The morning sun was pouring through the window.

Asleep. I'd been asleep.

I stretched my arms over my head and glanced around. My eyes stopped on the dummy. It sat slumped on the floor by my closet with its arms dangling to the rug and legs straight out. The glassy eyes stared down at his shoes.

"Slappy?" My voice was clogged from sleep.

The dummy didn't move.

"Whoa. What a dream!" I said out loud.

That whole thing with Slappy talking and telling me I'm now the Son of Slappy — it must have been a bad dream.

A chill ran down my back. It was such a strong, real dream.

I climbed out of bed and crossed the room. I hesitated for a moment. Then I kicked the dummy in the chest with my bare foot.

66

It bounced, then fell back in a heap. Lifeless.

The dummy wasn't alive. What a frightening, weird nightmare.

At breakfast, Mom and Dad both asked me why I was so cheerful today. "I've never seen anyone so cheerful in the morning. Maybe we should take you to the doctor," Mom joked.

I wanted to say, "I'm cheerful because the dummy isn't alive." But, of course, it wouldn't make any sense to them. So I just said I had a good sleep.

Rachel scowled across the breakfast table at me. "I still don't understand why Jack got a sweater, and I didn't get anything," she whined.

"Rachel, stop complaining," Dad said. "We told you. Aunt Ada is sending your present later."

"She never sends me anything good," Rachel said. "Last year, she sent me bright green socks. Why would anyone send green socks? I stuffed them in my bottom drawer so I wouldn't have to look at them."

"Rachel, forget the socks. Did you do your math assignment last night?" Mom demanded.

Rachel sighed. "Some of it."

"Some of it?"

"Well, Alyssa texted me and then we started talking and . . ."

Mom tsk-tsked. "Rachel, you promised. You promised you'd get your homework done."

67

Rachel grinned. "I had my fingers crossed when I promised."

I told you. She's a problem child.

Later, in art class, we were all working hard, painting posters for the YC bake sale and talent show. We sat at the long tables in the art room with our brushes and big jars of paint in front of us, sketching and painting.

Mr. Tallen, the art teacher, had dance music bombing from a big old boombox on his desk. Mr. Tallen says artists work better to music.

The pounding dance beat of the music kept the energy up. Everyone was bobbing their heads, bouncing along, working hard and having a good time.

"Dance . . . dance . . . dance to the music . . ."

I still felt cheerful. I love the smell of paint. And I was happy that everyone in my class was pitching in to help the YC. Maybe if we all worked really hard, the YC could stay open for another year.

I thought about Froggy and Nikki and all the kids. How happy they'd be to keep playing there after school.

I had a good idea for a funny skit. It would be about a bunch of kids trying to take care of two canaries. And, of course, they'd mess everything up.

And I kept thinking up jokes I could do at the show with Slappy. I really wanted to help Mrs. Pearson and everyone at the YC. I knew they were counting on me.

I leaned over my poster. I was painting a bright yellow sun and a smiling kid beneath it. And I planned to paint the words: *Keep the Kids Smiling.*

Suddenly, the music cut off. "Let's take a ten-minute break," Mr. Tallen said. "You can all go outside and relax for a few minutes. I'll join you."

There was a clatter of chairs, paintbrushes being set down, paint jars closing. Everyone was shouting and laughing. The room emptied out very quickly.

I glanced around. I was the only one who didn't leave. I just wanted to finish filling in the sun on my poster.

I slapped yellow paint on the posterboard. I smoothed my brush over it. I could hear the kids from my class outside the art room window.

Suddenly, I heard another sound. A *chirp*. A loud *chirp*. Then another.

My head — it suddenly felt so strange. The room started to tilt one way, then the other. I shut my eyes, but the dizziness wouldn't go away.

Then I heard a different noise. It was the

sound of Slappy's shrill cackle. Why did I hear that? Why did it feel like it was inside my head?

I held up my paintbrush. I didn't think about it. I just picked it up and dipped it into a jar of black paint.

So dizzy ... my head ... feels so HEAVY.

I raised the paintbrush and smeared thick lines of black paint all over my poster. More paint. More paint. I worked frantically until my poster was covered in black.

Then I dipped the brush again and painted black smears all over the poster next to mine. I reached across the table and ruined another poster, brushing thick black streaks over it ... more ... more.

This is AWESOME!

Did I really think that? Was that *me* thinking that?

Yessss! Awesome!

I picked up a jar of dark blue paint. I tilted it upside down and poured the paint all over the art table. Then I stood up, reached down, and painted the seat of my chair blue. I painted a few more chairs, slapping paint all over them. Faster ... more paint ...

Awesome! This is so totally AWESOME!

I took a jar of red paint and let it dribble onto the floor. Then I took another paint jar — purple — and splashed the paint against the wall.

Awesome!

I tossed back my head and let out a long laugh.

Oh, wow. My laugh was high and shrill — and as nasty as Slappy's.

I laughed and laughed. I laughed till my throat hurt. I couldn't stop.

But, wait.

I heard voices in the hall. The kids were all returning to the art room.

I stood and stared at the door.

Think fast, Jackson. Think fast.

How could I explain this mess?

18

The footsteps were right outside the door.

I took a paint jar and spilled red paint down the front of my T-shirt. Then I smeared some paint on my face.

Kids cried out in shock as they stepped into the room. Mr. Tallen went pale. He kept blinking fast and swallowing.

It took him a while to focus on me.

I went running toward him, my face twisted in alarm. "It was three dogs!" I cried. "Three huge dogs. They . . . they jumped in through the window!" I pointed to the open window.

I made a choking noise. I made my chest heave up and down.

"Calm down, Jackson," Mr. Tallon said. He put a hand on my shoulder. "Take a deep breath. Are you okay?"

"L-look what they did!" I stammered. "They jumped all over the tables and spilled paint everywhere. I — I tried to stop them. But there were *three* of them!"

"Funny. I didn't hear any barking." Mr. Tallon's eyes swept over the horrible mess on the table, the floor, the wall.

I took a few gasping breaths. The other kids stared at me. No one spoke or moved.

"They . . . just went nuts," I said in a trembling voice. "When I tried to grab them, they growled at me and snapped. It . . . it was pretty scary. I finally chased them back out the window."

Mr. Tallon walked to the window and peered out. "I don't see them now."

"I . . . I'm so sorry!" I cried. "Really. So . . . sorry . . ."

"It wasn't your fault," Mr. Tallon said. "I'm sure you did your best in a scary situation." He started toward the hall. "I'm going to alert the principal. Perhaps she'll want to call the town police."

I made my shoulders shake up and down. I tried to look as upset as I could.

Mr. Tallon turned at the door. "Jackson, do you have another T-shirt in your gym locker? You could change without having to go home."

"Okay," I said softly.

The teacher studied me. "The dogs didn't bite you — did they?"

I shook my head. "No. But they tried."

I followed him out the art room door. Then I turned and went down the stairs to the gym locker room.

Of course he believed my story, I thought. *He knows that Jackson Stander would never lie. I'm the most trusted kid in school.*

You bet.

I pulled open the door to the locker room. The aroma of sweat and dirty gym socks greeted me. The air was hot and damp.

Suddenly, I felt normal again.

I sucked in a deep breath. "What did I do?" I said out loud. My voice echoed down the empty rows of lockers. "Why did I do that?"

The answer came to me in a flash.

It was too horrible. Too frightening. Too impossible. But I knew it was true.

Slappy. Slappy got inside my head. Slappy made me destroy the posters and splash paint over the art room.

A chill made my whole body shudder. I hugged myself. I didn't want to believe it.

I was *possessed*!

He invaded my brain. It wasn't a dream. He was alive — and I was the Son of Slappy.

"Nooo." A moan escaped my throat.

I don't want to be Slappy's son. His slave. I don't want to be evil.

My hands were shaking hard as I changed into

74

my clean T-shirt. I tossed the paint-smeared shirt into a trash can.

I wanted to go home. I wanted to stand up to Slappy. I wanted to tell him, "Stop it! STOP it — right now!"

I wanted to shout, "Leave me ALONE! Stay out of my HEAD!"

No. Better than that. I decided to get rid of the dummy. Send him back to Grandpa Whitman? No. I wouldn't do something that horrible to my grandfather.

Edgar was right. He tried to warn me. If only I had listened.

Okay. I would take care of it. I would dump the dummy in a trash can somewhere far from my house.

That thought made me feel better. Only three more hours of school. Then I'd go home and say good-bye forever to Slappy.

I shut my gym locker and checked my watch. Art class was over. I headed back to my regular classroom. Miss Hathaway, my teacher, wasn't at her desk.

I glanced around the room. The kids were all reading from the science textbook. No one looked up when I stepped into the room. Not even Stick and Miles.

Miles had his face covered by his book. Sometimes he takes short naps, and Miss Hathaway never guesses.

"Oh." I muttered a startled cry.

I heard the *chirp* sound again. Just a quiet *chirp*, not loud enough to make any of the kids glance up from their reading.

I glanced around the room again. I wanted to find what made that sound.

But no time. I felt a tingle in my head. Like a buzzing. The room went cloudy for a moment, then bright again.

I started to walk past Miss Hathaway's desk. I saw her red-framed eyeglasses on top of her assignment book. Her brown canvas pocketbook. A blue-and-white scarf thrown over the back of her chair.

Then something caught my eye on the corner of her desk.

What was that? I squinted hard. The History test for tomorrow?

Just sitting there. Out where anyone could take it.

I chuckled to myself. I made sure no one was watching. Then I grabbed the test, rolled it into a tube, and carried it to my seat near the back of the room.

I stuffed it into my backpack. Two seconds later, Miss Hathaway walked into the room.

She is very tall and very thin and very pretty. She has wavy blond hair and blue eyes and a great smile. She wears dark sweaters and short skirts over black tights. Everyone thinks she's the coolest teacher in school.

"Everybody is reading quietly," she said. "I'm impressed."

She sat down at her desk. She moved her glasses and set her canvas bag on the floor.

Then she turned and gazed down at her desk. She shifted in her chair. And then she turned to me.

"Jackson?" she called.

My breath caught in my throat.

Oh, no. Caught.

19

"Jackson?" she repeated.

I lowered my eyes to my backpack. *Maybe I can tell her I picked up the test by accident.*

"Jackson, I understand you had a very scary experience in the art room," Miss Hathaway said.

"Uh . . . yeah," I murmured.

"Are you feeling okay? If you'd like to go take a short rest in the nurse's office . . ."

I let out a long breath. *She didn't see me take the test.*

"No, I'm fine," I said. "Just a little shaky. But I'm okay."

Everyone was looking at me now. "I'll probably have nightmares about dogs tonight," I said. "Dogs with big paintbrushes."

It was a lame joke, but a few kids laughed.

Miss Hathaway smiled — but her expression suddenly changed. Her eyes went wide, and her mouth dropped open. She was staring at the spot where the History test had rested.

"Uh-oh," she said. "Uh-oh." She jumped to her feet. Her face turned bright red. She drummed the desk with her fingers.

"The History test for tomorrow seems to be missing," she said through clenched teeth. I could see she was trying to stay calm. But she was angry and upset and couldn't hide it.

Her eyes swept the room. She was going from face to face.

"I'm sure someone picked it up by accident," she said. "If you'd like to return it now, I won't say another word about it."

Kids mumbled and whispered.

Across the room, I saw Stick give Miles a shove. "Go ahead, Miles. Give it back," he said.

Everyone turned to them. Stick tossed his hands up. "Joking!" he said. "Just joking."

Miles punched Stick in the ribs. "How funny was *that*?"

"That was a lame joke, Mickey," Miss Hathaway scolded him. "This is a serious matter. Stealing a test from a teacher's desk is serious. It's a school crime. You can be suspended for doing this."

The room grew silent again.

My head buzzed. I felt as if I were gazing through clouds.

Miss Hathaway pressed both hands on her desk. "I'm going to ask one more time," she said. "If you took the test, bring it up here and no questions will be asked."

79

No one moved.

She drummed her fingernails on the desk. She turned to Clay Dobbs. Clay is like my sister, Rachel — always in trouble. There's one in every class.

"Clay?" Miss Hathaway said, giving him the evil eye. "Do you have something you want to tell me?"

Clay let out a bleating sound. Like a sheep caught in a fence. "No way!" he cried. "Why are you looking at *me*?"

Miss Hathaway raised her eyes to Stick and Miles. "You boys were joking, right? You didn't really take the test, did you, Miles?"

Miles shook his head. "I get A's in history," he said. "No way I need to cheat."

"Then who took it? Come on. Somebody confess." Miss Hathaway's eyes moved slowly from face to face.

She didn't even glance at me. She knew Jackson Stander would *never* steal a test. She knew what a good, honest dude I am.

As I watched her, I had to laugh. *Ha-ha. Too bad for you losers. I'll get an easy A tomorrow. I'll get every single answer right.*

Whoa. Wait. I suddenly realized the kids were all staring at me. Miss Hathaway, too.

Oh, no. They were staring at me because I was *cackling at the top of my lungs.*

20

I hurried home after school. Stick and Miles wanted to hang out. But I told them I had too much homework.

My brain felt normal. I wanted to take care of my Slappy problem while I still felt like myself.

I heard voices in the den, but I didn't stop to say hi. I ran up the stairs and into my room. I closed the door behind me.

Slappy sat on my bed, just where I'd left him that morning. He opened his eyes wide when I walked in and tilted his big head toward me.

"How's it going, Son?" he called in his high, tinny voice.

"Don't call me that!" I screamed. "Don't ever call me son!"

"Tell me, Son, did you get my signal?"

I scowled at him. "I got your signal. I heard

your stupid chirp. You made me wreck all the YC posters and the art room. And you made me steal a test."

He tossed back his head and laughed. "That's a start, Son."

"No — not a start!" I cried. "That's the *end*. I mean it, Slappy. Stay out of my head. You can't do that to me again!"

I tried to sound tough, but my voice trembled and cracked.

His eyes shut, then quickly opened. "The fun hasn't started, Son. Today was just practice."

"Noooo!" I let out a cry and dove toward him. I had the sudden urge to pick him up and tear him to pieces.

But before I reached the bed, I heard that sound again. A loud *chirp*.

I staggered to a stop. I suddenly felt too dizzy to walk. The ceiling and floor appeared to be closing in on each other.

I shook my head hard, trying to shake the weird feeling away.

And then I heard my mom's voice shouting up from downstairs. "Jackson? Are you home? Come down and say hi. Aunt Ada, Uncle Josh, and your cousin Noah are here."

I groaned. Cousin Noah? He was eight and he acted like he was two. I hated to eat dinner with him. He always had food stuck to his teeth. And he whined all the time, whined like a baby.

But I had no choice. I turned away from Slappy and started out of my room. I was heading down the hall when I heard his raspy shout:

"Have a great dinner, Son."

21

I hurried downstairs. Everyone was already sitting at the dining room table.

I hugged Aunt Ada and shook hands with Uncle Josh. Noah stuck his tongue out at me and made a spitting sound.

"Noah, is that the way you say hi to your cousin?" Aunt Ada scolded him.

He laughed. "Yes." Then he spit again.

Uncle Josh just shook his head. He and Aunt Ada are like opposites. She's skinny and talks all the time. He's pretty fat and almost never says a word. I always think they're like salt and pepper. In fact, she has black hair, and his hair is white.

Noah has a round baby face, short brown hair like fuzz on an egg, and two front teeth that stick out and make him look like Bugs Bunny. He always wears a baggy T-shirt and cargo shorts. He doesn't like long pants.

I took my seat next to Rachel. She was tapping her spoon on her bowl, waiting for the soup to be poured. Rachel gets very impatient at mealtime.

Mom served the soup. Then she said, "Jackson, tell Aunt Ada how much you like the sweater she bought you."

I opened my mouth to speak — but my head felt heavy. I felt very strange.

"It's a terrific sweater," I told my aunt. "I don't wear it. I use it as a snot rag."

"As a *what*?" Aunt Ada's mouth dropped open.

"Yeah, I blow my nose in it," I said.

Noah was the only one who laughed. Dad dropped his soup spoon. Rachel stared at me as if I was some kind of weird animal species.

Mom squinted at me. "Jackson? Was that a joke?"

"Your *soup* is a joke," I said. "I've puked up better food than this!"

Mom gasped and nearly fell off her chair. Noah started to choke on his soup. Aunt Ada slapped his back.

I'm saying these horrible things, and I can't help myself.

Slappy is in my head. He is totally controlling me. These are his horrible jokes, and he's forcing me to say them.

I couldn't stop myself. I held up a spoonful of

85

the pea soup. "I've seen better looking scabs," I said.

I turned to Uncle Josh. "Are you really that fat?" I said. "Or does someone inflate you in the morning? Didn't I see you in the Thanksgiving parade?"

He scowled at me. He gazed at my mother. I could see he was confused.

"I'm sorry," I told him. "You're not fat. You're TOO BIG to be fat. Where do you shop for clothes? Piggly Wiggly?"

Aunt Ada jumped to her feet. She bumped her soup bowl, and soup splashed onto the tablecloth.

"Jackson — this isn't like you at all," she cried. "I can't believe you're so rude."

"I can't believe you're so ugly," I said. "Do you have to take *lessons* to be that ugly?"

"That's enough!" Mom screamed. She jumped to her feet and rushed over to me. She put a hand on my forehead. "This isn't like you at all. There's something very wrong. Are you sick?"

I brushed her hand away. "Get used to it," I said. "Like I had to get used to your chimpanzee face. Did you always look like that? Or were you in a bad car accident?"

I turned to my dad. "You like horror movies. Have you looked in a mirror lately?"

"Jackson, stop!" he screamed. "Did someone dare you to insult everyone?"

"Did someone dare you to be so stupid?" I replied. "You're thirty-six, right? But is that your age or your IQ?"

I dipped my spoon into my pea soup and sent a glob of soup flying across the table into Noah's face. Noah uttered a startled cry.

Now, everyone was on their feet. Mom and Dad each took a shoulder and pushed me out of the dining room. "Have you gone crazy?" Dad demanded. "*Have* you?"

"Should I call the doctor?" Mom asked in a trembling voice.

"He's bad. He's gone bad!" Rachel cried. I could see the big smile on her face.

Dad guided me to the stairs. "Just go to your room. Stay up there till you're ready to come back and apologize."

"Don't hold your breath," I said.

They watched me climb the stairs. They were all muttering and shaking their heads in shock.

I slumped into my room. My head felt about to explode. All the horrible things I'd said kept repeating in my mind.

I raised my eyes to Slappy, perched on my bed. He grinned at me. "How was dinner, Son?"

22

I threw myself across the room and grabbed Slappy by the shoulders. I shook him, shook him hard.

A giggle escaped his open mouth.

I tossed him back against the wall. My chest was heaving. I could barely breathe. "Don't call me *son*," I said.

He giggled again.

How can this be happening? He's just a doll. He's made of wood and plastic.

I could hear voices from downstairs. Everyone was talking at once.

"Listen to them," I said. "Listen to how upset they are. They want to take me to a doctor. They know I don't act like that. They know I couldn't mean those things," I said.

"Tough beans," the dummy muttered.

"Why?" I cried. "Why are you making me do these horrible things?"

His eyes blinked. "Evil is its own reward," he said. "Relax, Son. You'll learn to love it!"

"Noooo!" I shouted. "No, I won't. You've got to stop. You've got to leave me alone!"

"Calm down, Son," the dummy said. "I'm proud of you. You've come a long way. You were the best, nicest, sweetest kid in the world. And now you're as sick and twisted as I am." He chuckled. "That's something to be proud of."

"No. No way —" I started to protest. "You can't —"

I heard a *chirp*. The room appeared to shake.

Perched on the bed, Slappy tossed his head back. He opened his wooden mouth wide and began to laugh.

And . . . and . . . I couldn't help myself. I couldn't control myself.

I tossed back my head — and I laughed with him.

I laughed and laughed. Crazy, horrible laughter.

I couldn't stop even when I saw someone in the bedroom doorway.

Rachel. Standing at the door. Squinting hard at me, hands on her waist, as I laughed along with the dummy.

I didn't stop until she cried out in alarm: "Jackson — what's so funny?"

23

I swallowed. My throat was dry from laughing.

I forced myself away from the bed. I hurtled across the room. I grabbed my sister by the arm and pulled her into the hall.

"This — this is all *your* fault!" I cried breathlessly.

She tugged my hand off her arm. "Let go of me. Are you crazy? Mom wants to call Dr. Marx. Aunt Ada thinks you should go to the emergency room."

"All your fault," I repeated, trying to clear my mind.

"Jackson, what are you talking about?" Rachel demanded. "What did I do?"

"You shouted out those words," I said. "You brought the dummy to life."

She flattened her back against the wall. She blinked a few times, then stared at me. "You really have gone nuts. . . ."

"No. I'm serious. It's true," I insisted.

I pointed toward my room. "Didn't you see him in there? Didn't you see him laughing his head off?"

"I only saw you," she said.

"Well, he's alive," I said. "You brought him to life. He's alive, and he's evil, and —"

Rachel backed away. "I think I'm scared of you, Jackson. Really."

"Listen to me," I cried. "I swear I'm telling the truth. I'm not crazy, Rachel. That dummy —"

"That dummy is a copy," Rachel said. "It isn't even the real Slappy. You heard what Grandpa Whitman said."

"Grandpa Whitman was wrong," I told her. "This is the real Slappy. This is the totally evil dummy he told us about."

She stared at me and didn't reply. I could see her thinking hard.

"It — it's making me do all those horrible things," I stammered. "He says I'm his son now, and —"

"His son?"

I nodded. "He — he made me say all those horrible rude insults. He's totally gross, and he's making *me* totally gross. He's using *me* as a dummy."

Rachel shook her head. "How?" she demanded. "How is he doing that?"

"He's inside my head," I explained. "I hear a sound and then there he is. He's in my brain!"

"Really. You're scaring me," Rachel said. "Did you hit your head or something? Did you fall down and hit your head?"

I let out a long sigh. "No, I didn't hit my head. Rachel, you know me. I — I'm not crazy. I don't insult people. Never. I don't play practical jokes, right? And I always tell the truth."

She studied my face. Finally, she said, "Yeah. That's true. You don't make things up."

"So you believe me?"

She grabbed my arm and tugged me toward the bedroom door. "You've never lied to me before. Not once. So go ahead. Show me, Jackson. Prove it to me. Show me he's alive."

"Okay," I said. I led her up to the bed. "Okay. Okay. Here goes. Stand back and watch."

24

The dummy sat with its legs straight out across my bed. Its back was pressed against the wall. Its head slumped forward, and its arms dangled loosely, folded on the bedspread.

"Slappy, sit up," I said. "Explain to Rachel."

The dummy didn't move.

"Slappy, tell Rachel who the Son of Slappy is," I demanded.

The dummy remained hunched over, limp and lifeless.

"Come on, Slappy. I know you're awake," I said. "Come on, move."

No. He didn't budge.

I picked him up and shook him. "Wake up, Slappy. Stop this. Wake up and talk to Rachel."

The legs flew about loosely as I shook him. The arms dangled limply. The head flopped forward.

"Talk! Talk! Talk!" I screamed.

I felt Rachel's hand on my arm. "Put it down. Come on, Jackson. Put it down. Shaking it isn't going to do anything."

With an angry cry, I tossed the dummy onto the bed. It landed on its back. Its head and hands bounced up once, then settled lifelessly on the bedspread.

I was breathing hard. My heart pounded in my chest.

Rachel stared down at the dummy. Then she raised her eyes to me. "Jackson . . . I . . . don't understand."

I heard a loud *chirp*.

Rachel became all fuzzy, like a photo out of focus. Then she slowly became sharp again.

My head felt strange . . . heavy.

"Of *course* you don't understand," I snapped. "You need a *brain* to understand."

"Jackson —"

"Rachel, remember that test you took in school? It said you have the same IQ as a cantaloupe?"

She slapped my shoulder. "Shut up. Why are you being so horrible?"

"A cantaloupe is better looking," I said. "The skin is so much nicer. If I had your face, I'd walk on my hands. Let people see my better end!"

I tossed back my head and laughed a cold, cruel laugh.

"Just shut up. You're a jerk!"

I pushed her back a few inches. "Could you step away? Your breath is curling the wallpaper. Ever hear of a thing called a toothbrush?"

"Aaaaagh!" She let out an angry growl. "I hate you. I really do. I'm going to tell Mom and Dad how mean you were to me." She shoved me aside and stormed to the stairs.

"I was just telling the truth!" I shouted. Then I tossed back my head and laughed again.

I was still laughing when Slappy suddenly jerked to life. He raised his head and straightened his back. His big wooden hand shot out quickly — and he grabbed my arm.

"Owww." I let out a howl of pain as the wooden fingers tightened around my arm. Tighter . . . tighter. Pain roared up my entire right side.

"Ohhhh. Stop. Let go."

But the hard hand refused to loosen its grip.

"You made a bad mistake, Son," the dummy rasped in its ugly, shrill voice. "You should *never* tell others about me."

"But — but —"

He brought his head close to mine and shouted in my ear. "That makes me very unhappy, Son. You don't want to see me when I'm unhappy — *do* you?"

25

The next morning, I didn't want to go down to breakfast. I knew I'd have to explain to Mom and Dad why I went berserk at dinner.

But could I tell them the truth?

No way. If I explained about Slappy, they wouldn't believe me. They would want to drag me to a doctor. And it would make Slappy angry at me again.

He was right. I didn't want to see him angry. Just thinking about it sent a cold shiver down my back.

"Jackson?" I heard Mom calling from downstairs. "Come down to breakfast. You're going to be late for school."

I had no choice. I made my way slowly down the stairs and into the kitchen.

Rachel sat at the table, a bowl of Frosted Flakes in front of her. She had an orange-juice mustache on her upper lip.

Dad's plate just had crumbs and a puddle of syrup. That meant he had already gone to work.

Mom studied me as I entered. She was still in her pink bathrobe. She held a coffee mug in both hands. She tapped her foot nervously.

"Jackson?"

"I can explain," I said. "You see, I had a bad headache last night, and —"

I'm such a bad liar.

I'm used to telling the truth all the time. I'm a real good dude, remember?

Mom squinted at me. "A headache? I'm afraid that doesn't explain your incredible rudeness."

I lowered my head. "I know," I murmured. "But you see —"

"Did you suddenly think that you were a comedian?" Mom said. "Did you think all those crude insults were *funny*?"

I kept my eyes on the floor. "Not really."

"I can tell you about funny," Mom said, growing more angry. "I know about funny. And making fun of people's looks and hurting their feelings —"

"I know," I repeated. "I didn't mean it. I can't really explain it. I —"

"That was just awful," Mom said. Her hand trembled as she set her coffee mug down. Her eyes glistened. Did she have tears in them?

"I'm sorry," I murmured.

97

"Your aunt and uncle were just horrified," she said. "They know what a good guy you are. The things you said to them were unforgivable, Jackson. Do you hear me? Unforgivable."

I glanced at Rachel at the table. She had a huge grin on her face. She was really enjoying this. Really *loving* seeing me be the bad guy for once.

"You were so awful," Mom continued in a tense, tight voice. "Your father and I don't have a clue as to what your punishment should be. But you need to learn that you can't talk to people that way."

"He was mean to me, too!" Rachel chimed in.

Mom bit her lips. "Yes. And then you went upstairs and were mean to your sister. You didn't quit. You had to be horrible to her, too."

I have to tell her the truth. I have no choice. I have to tell her about how Slappy is controlling me.

Otherwise, she'll think I've turned into some kind of a monster.

I took a deep breath and started. "Mom, I have to explain something."

That's as far as I got when I heard a sharp *chirp*.

The room tilted. Shadows slid over the kitchen. Then it became bright again. My mind suddenly felt strange. . . .

Oh NO! What am I going to do now?

26

I froze.

Mom stared at me. "Jackson? What did you want to tell me?"

"Uh . . ." I hesitated. Then the words came from somewhere deep in my brain. "I just wanted to say that your face looks like something I pulled out of the garbage disposal."

"Huh?" She gasped. I saw her hands tighten into fists.

"But no one notices your face because you smell so bad," I said.

Mom's eyes bulged. Her mouth was open, but no sound came out.

"Jackson — shut up. What's your problem?" Rachel cried.

I spun around to face her. "Hey, I wrote a song for you," I said. "It describes you perfectly."

I took a breath and started to grunt. *"Oink oink oink oinnnk."* I grunted like a pig.

"But cheer up," I said. "You're not a fat pig. You're just an ugly, hairy pig."

I tossed back my head and laughed.

"Jackson — *stop*!" Mom screamed. "Don't say another word. I mean it. Not another word."

I nodded. I took my fingers and made a zipping motion over my lips.

"That's better," Mom said. "We have to figure out what's wrong with you. I'm not sure I can let you go to school like this."

"He's crazy," Rachel said. "Last night he told me that dummy was making him say the bad things."

Mom squinted at Rachel. "The dummy? That's crazy. How could a dummy make Jackson say all those horrible things?"

Rachel grinned. She was enjoying this *too much*. "He says the dummy is alive," she told Mom. "I told you — he's gone nutso."

Mom let out a long sigh. Her hands were still balled into tight fists. I could see how worried she was.

But what could I do? I wasn't in control.

I walked to the breakfast table and picked up Rachel's cereal bowl. Then I dumped it over her head.

Rachel screamed.

I watched the mushy clumps of cereal run down her hair and the sides of her face.

100

Mom grabbed me by the shoulders. "That's the last straw!" She pushed me toward the door. "Go up to your room — now. Stay in there. I'm going to call your father. He and I have to discuss what to do with you."

I started to the hall. But I turned back at the doorway and gazed at Rachel. *"Oink oink oink,"* I grunted.

Mom hurried to the table to help pull the clumps of cereal from Rachel's hair. She and Rachel weren't watching, so I stopped at the pantry. I grabbed Rachel's jar of honey and carried it upstairs with me.

In my room, I found the new sweater Aunt Ada gave me. I spread it out on my bed. Then I opened the jar and poured the honey all over the sweater.

What a mess.

I set the jar down on the floor. Then I ran to the head of the stairs.

"Mom!" I shouted. "Mom! I don't believe it! Hurry. Come quick! Look what Rachel did to my new sweater!"

27

Well, guess what? Mom didn't believe for one second that Rachel poured the honey on my sweater.

She gasped in horror when she saw it. She was so upset, I saw tears in her eyes. Rachel stood in the doorway, shaking her head. I think even *she* was upset about what I had done.

Instead of yelling at me, Mom hugged me. "What is wrong, Jackson?" she said softly. "Can you tell me why you're doing and saying these horrible things?"

I glimpsed Slappy, perched on the bed with that red-lipped grin frozen on his face. I was desperate to tell Mom the truth. Desperate to tell her that Slappy was alive and inside my head, making me do and say things I didn't want to.

But who would believe that story?

I just shrugged and didn't answer.

The next few days were not pleasant. Mom and Dad took me to see our family doctor. They wanted Dr. Marx to give me pills to calm me down. The doctor talked to me for an hour and decided I should stay home for a few days and just relax.

In other words, I was totally grounded. I couldn't go to school. And I couldn't go to the YC to help the kids work on their skit.

I stayed in my room, playing games on my game-player until my thumbs were red and sore.

Stick brought me my homework every afternoon so I wouldn't get behind. Miss Hathaway even came to visit one afternoon to tell me about things that were going on at school.

All week, my parents kept squinting at me day and night. Studying me like I was some kind of weird alien species. They were so totally tense, they watched my every move. Really. Once, I burped — and they both jumped.

I guess they expected me to go berserk again. Me? I didn't know *what* to expect.

I carried Slappy to my clothes closet and sat him in a corner. Then I covered him in an old bedsheet. I made sure the closet door was shut tight.

I knew he could get out if he wanted to. But he didn't move at all while I was grounded. And he stayed out of my mind and didn't make me say anything horrible.

My parents were so happy that I seemed normal again, they let me go to the YC to help the kids with their skit.

Yes, it was nearly time for the big YC bake sale and show. Everyone was counting on me. The skit was going well. And I had promised I'd do a comedy act with Slappy.

But how could I bring that evil thing to the YC?

I didn't know. I didn't want to think about it.

But I kept wondering if maybe I could make a deal with Slappy. Promise him something in return for his being quiet at the YC show. Maybe promise I'd be a perfect son if he swore he wouldn't ruin the whole night.

Stick, Miles, and I still hadn't decided what to bake for the big bake sale competition. We were going to have a big meeting at Stick's house to decide.

Mom and Dad discussed it. They didn't really want me to go to Stick's. They still wanted to keep me home, where they could watch me.

But I pleaded with them. I told them how much everyone at the YC was counting on me to help keep the YC alive. And I reminded them I'd been good for days.

Finally, they agreed to let me go to Stick's house for a few hours.

"I promise I won't get in any trouble," I said, raising my right hand to swear. "I promise I'll be just like the old me."

Think I was able to keep that promise?

28

It was a warm, sunny day with a few puffy clouds high in the sky. The sunshine felt good on my face as I walked to Stick's house.

It had poured down rain the night before. The sidewalks and the street still had deep puddles, and the grass gleamed wetly.

A black cat ran right in front of me as I turned the corner. But I didn't care. I felt so lucky to be out of the house and out in the sunshine. And I felt lucky to feel like my old self.

Stick, Miles, and I still had a problem. We hadn't thought up a better idea for what to bake. The giant cupcake was our most awesome idea. But of course, it was impossible.

I was thinking about cookies and cakes when I saw the little kid near the curb. He was about seven or eight. He had curly blond hair and a round red face. His black T-shirt came down nearly to the knees of his cargo jeans.

He was bent over his bike, tugging at the handlebars, making loud groaning sounds with each tug.

I hurried over to him. "Can I help?" I said. "What's the problem?"

"It's stuck," he groaned. "My bike. I'm late for my tennis lesson. But my bike got stuck in the mud."

"Stand back." I pushed him gently to the side. "I'll get it out. No problem."

"Hey, thanks," he said. He was breathing hard, and his face was still red from all the tugging.

I grabbed the handlebars and started to pull. But then I heard a loud *chirp*.

I let go of the handlebars. The sky darkened for a second. And it felt like the ground was shaking under my feet.

I turned from the bike. "Can I see your tennis racket?" I said.

The boy pointed to the basket on the front of the bike. I lifted the racket case from the basket.

I opened the case and slid out the tennis racket. "Nice," I said. "Is it titanium?"

The little guy nodded.

I swung the racket hard and jammed the head deep in the mud.

"Hey!" The boy let out a cry.

Then I tugged the bike up from the mud. I raised it over my head in both hands — and *heaved* it into the street.

Then I dipped my hands into the mud. I swung around and wiped mud all over the boy's face.

He screamed again and twisted away.

I tossed back my head and uttered a long Slappy laugh.

The boy started to cry. That made me laugh even harder.

Then I took off running. My feet slapped the sidewalk as I ran.

I gasped when I heard a man's booming shout: "Hey, you! Come back here!"

I turned my head and saw Mr. Gurewitz, our neighbor.

He saw me. He saw what I did.

Now what?

29

"Come back here!" Gurewitz shouted.

I turned and ran toward the nearest house. I pushed open the wooden gate and darted along the garage to the backyard.

I could hear Gurewitz's heavy footsteps. He was chasing after me. "Come back! Stop! I saw you!"

I ducked my head under a volleyball net and ran into the next yard. A man was watering his garden with a long hose. He had his back turned and didn't see me as I crossed to the next house.

"Stop right there!" Mr. Gurewitz's shout made the man spin around, and a powerful stream of water sprayed Gurewitz from head to foot.

Gurewitz cried out in shock. He stopped running.

I glimpsed him wiping water off his face as I turned and ducked along the side of a house. I made it to the street and kept running.

No sign of Gurewitz. I guess his cold shower made him give up.

I started to feel like myself again as I crossed the street onto Stick's block. Two kids passed by on bikes. Both of them wore blue baseball caps and had iPod buds in their ears. They didn't turn to look at me.

I stopped to catch my breath. I felt bad about the little boy with the tennis racket. How could I do such a mean thing?

Did Mr. Gurewitz recognize me? He only saw me from the back. But he probably knew it was me. That meant he would probably tell my parents.

And then . . . I was doomed.

I tried not to think about it as Stick greeted me at his front door. "Yo, what's up?"

"Not much," I said. I pictured the tennis racket jammed deep in the mud. "I'm feeling okay. Think I can go back to school on Monday."

Miles popped up from the living room couch. "What for?" he asked. "You got it made, dude. You get to stay home all day." He laughed.

"It's way boring," I said. I glimpsed the time display on the cable box on top of the TV. "Hey, let's get going," I said. "I'm only allowed to stay an hour or so. My parents are still on my case."

"That's cuz you're a mental case!" Miles said.

"Not funny," Stick said. "That's not cool, Miles. Jackson isn't a mental case. He's a *nut* case."

They both laughed. Stick's mom walked into the room.

"What are you guys laughing about?" she asked. "Did someone burp?"

"Mom, give us a break," Stick groaned. "We're a little more sophisticated than that."

Miles burped really loud, and we all laughed.

"You three are going to turn my kitchen into a disaster zone," she said. "Will I need to hose it down when you're finished?"

My heart skipped a beat. I thought of Mr. Gurewitz getting the hose spray in the face.

"No. We'll be neat," Stick told her. "I promise. We'll clean it up perfectly when we're done."

"First we have to decide what to bake," Miles said.

"Your giant cupcake idea was a real loser," Mrs. Haggerty said.

"Thanks for the support, Mom." Stick rolled his eyes.

"I know," Miles said, jumping to his feet. "Why not bake regular cupcakes? We could do dozens of them. Maybe make the icing all different colors. Maybe the icing spells out something when they're on the tray?"

"Cool," I said. "Maybe put *Y*'s and *C*'s on the icing. You know. For YC?"

"You're a good speller," Mrs. Haggerty joked. "Okay, guys. Have fun. Just don't make my kitchen look like a tsunami rolled over it. I'm serious."

We watched her walk out of the room. Then we made our way to the kitchen.

It took us a while to find a nice, easy cupcake recipe in Mrs. Haggerty's collection of cookbooks. Then we scrambled around the kitchen in search of the ingredients for the cake batter.

"Have you ever baked anything before?" I asked my two friends.

They both shook their heads. "I made Cheerios once," Miles said. "That's all I ever made."

"It's easy," Stick said, pouring flour into a big mixing bowl. "You just follow the recipe step by step. You can't mess up."

We poured a bunch of ingredients into the mixing bowl. Then we put the bowl under the mixer and started the blades whirring.

"It's like magic!" Miles exclaimed. "Like science fiction or something. Look. It's turning into chocolate cake batter."

I sniffed it. "Smells like chocolate cake, too. This is totally awesome."

Stick pulled cupcake pans from the cabinet. Each pan held six cupcakes. "We have to make a lot," he said. "No one will be impressed if we walk in with twelve cupcakes. We need a hundred!"

I shook my head. "I don't think we have enough batter." All three of us stared into the bowl. The thick chocolate glop looked about ready to pour into the baking trays.

"Tell you what," Stick said. "Miles and I will run to Garrity's on the corner. We'll buy cake batter mixes. It'll take five minutes." He pointed to the bowl. "You stay and mix, Jackson."

And that's what happened. Stick got his wallet. Then he and Miles ran to the store. I stood at the mixer, watching it slowly fold the chocolate batter.

And then, a few seconds after my friends were out the door, I heard a loud *chirp*.

"Oh nooo," I groaned.

The room shook. The floor tilted up, then down.

"No. Please. Please. No."

I struggled. I tried to fight it. But I wasn't strong enough.

I had to give in.

I'm the Son of Slappy. I can't stop myself!

30

I clicked off the mixer and pulled the big bowl of chocolate batter out from under it. I set the bowl down on the kitchen table.

Then, giggling to myself, I dipped my hand into the batter. I grabbed a big, gooey hunk of the chocolate stuff. Then I crossed the room and smeared it all over the yellow-and-white wallpaper.

I scooped out another handful of batter and smeared it on the side of the fridge. Then another big hunk of batter. And another. I spread them over the table and along the wall.

I couldn't stop laughing. This was so much fun!

I grabbed a blob of batter and tossed it onto the ceiling. Then I smeared chocolate over the kitchen cabinet doors.

"Yes! Yes! Beautiful!" A long, cruel laugh burst from deep in my throat.

The big bowl was almost empty. I'd smeared the batter all over the room. Breathing hard from excitement, I stuck my head in the bowl and licked batter off the sides.

"Yes! Delicious! Yes!"

I made loud animal noises as I licked up the sweet batter. I knew I had chocolate all over my face, but I didn't care.

Finally, I took the bowl and heaved it across the room. It bounced off the sink and clattered over the floor.

I stood there, licking chocolate off my lips and admiring my work. I whirled around when I heard a gasp behind me.

Mrs. Haggerty stood in the kitchen doorway, her mouth open in horror. Her eyes darted around the kitchen.

"Uh ... how long have you been standing there?" I asked.

She replied through gritted teeth. "Long enough, Jackson." And then a sharp cry burst from her throat. "Have you gone crazy? Are you *sick*?"

"I can explain," I said.

31

"Huh?" She swallowed hard. Her whole body was trembling. "Explain?"

I nodded. "Yes. See, I was just redecorating your kitchen. I think it's an improvement — don't you?"

I tossed back my head and laughed.

She opened her mouth to speak, but no sound came out. Finally, she uttered a shrill scream.

"If you don't like it, just say so," I told her.

After that, things happened fast. She grabbed me by the shoulders and pushed me out the back door. Next thing I knew, I was seated beside her in her car.

Then I was home. Then Mrs. Haggerty was facing my mom, squealing and squawking and exploding with anger. She was talking so fast and in such a high voice, I held my hands over my ears.

"Jackson, is this true?" My mom kept repeating, "Is this true? Is this true?"

She apologized a hundred times to Stick's mom. She offered to help clean up the mess. Mrs. Haggerty flashed me a concerned look. Then she hurried out, shaking her head.

Their words became a buzzing in my ears. My head spun.

I could feel Slappy moving out. Leaving my mind. I felt myself returning to normal. And as I did, I finally realized the horrible thing I'd done. And the horrible trouble I was in.

Dad came home from work early. His face was pale and grim. "Jackson, Mr. Gurewitz called me," Dad said. "He told me some terrible things about you. He said he saw you go berserk with a little boy's bike."

He stared at me, waiting for me to say something. But I didn't know how to reply. I just lowered my eyes and stared at the rug.

"Well, is it true?" Dad demanded. "Is it true that you smashed a little boy's tennis racket and threw his bike in the street?"

"I . . . guess," I muttered.

"I just got off the phone with Dr. Marx," Mom said, returning to the room. "He said he can see you right away."

"But, Mom —"

"No arguments, Jackson."

"Let's all stay calm," Dad said, motioning with both hands. I could see he wasn't calm at all. "You're acting very strange, and you know it.

116

The things you've done and the things you've said — they're not like you at all, Jackson."

"Don't worry. We'll take care of you," Mom said. "You'll be back to normal in no time." She glanced at Dad. I could see she didn't believe what she was saying.

I wanted to tell them about Slappy. I wanted to say if we just got rid of that dummy, maybe he'd stay out of my mind.

But I suddenly thought about the play rehearsal at the YC.

"I . . . I'm late for rehearsal," I stammered. "The YC show is in a few days, and —"

"I'm sorry, Jackson," Dad said softly. "I'm afraid you'll have to miss the YC show."

32

I'm going to skip to the night of the YC show because the past few days weren't interesting at all. Mostly, I clumped around the house feeling sorry for myself.

Dr. Marx gave me some blue pills to take that were supposed to mellow me out. But I only pretended to take them.

Rachel was being nice to me for a change. Actually, she was in a very good mood. I think she definitely enjoyed being the good kid in the family.

She came into my room and sat down on the edge of the bed. "I'm really sorry you're missing the YC show tonight," she said. "You must be very sad about it."

I nodded. "Yes. Very sad."

She glanced around my room. "Where is that dummy?"

"I stuffed him in the closet," I said. "I wanted

to do a comedy act with him tonight at the YC. But since I'm not allowed to go . . ."

"At least you feel okay — right?"

I couldn't believe she was being so nice to me. I felt bad that I was lying to her.

Lying about staying home and missing the YC show. *No way* would I miss that show tonight.

I couldn't let all the kids down. I couldn't let Mrs. Lawson and the YC people down. I *had* to be there. I had to be there to help with the play the kids were performing. And to do my comedy act with Slappy.

Yes, I planned to sneak out of the house.

I'd been thinking about it since I'd been grounded. I planned to sneak out and run to the YC.

And I wasn't worried about Slappy. I wasn't worried about that dummy slipping into my mind and making me evil.

I'd finally figured out how to defeat him. How to keep him from turning me into his dummy.

It was so totally simple.

All I had to do was stop his chirp. He hypnotized me with that chirp so he could take over my brain. That chirp was the signal that I was about to become his slave, his son.

And where did the chirp come from? It took me so long to figure it out. But I finally realized the chirp had to come from my game-player. Yes, the game-player I carried with me wherever I went.

Chirping Chickens. That was the game I always played. And that's where the chirp signal came from.

So how easy was it to tuck the game-player deep in a dresser drawer?

No problem.

And now the dummy had no power over me. He couldn't signal me. And if he couldn't give me the signal, he was helpless to control me.

Score one for Jackson!

I grabbed Slappy and lifted him out of my closet. His eyes were glassy, lifeless. He slumped limply under my arm.

"You have no power over me," I said. "You cannot signal me. You cannot do *anything* to me."

I tossed him over my shoulder, took a deep breath — and sneaked out of the house.

33

I ran all the way to the YC and crept in through the back door. I stepped into the backstage area of the auditorium. I dropped Slappy against the wall and peeked out through the side of the curtain.

Wow. The auditorium was full. A huge crowd. Awesome.

The show had already begun. A jazz band was playing, and a tall blond boy was bobbing up and down, blowing a wild saxophone. The golden horn glowed in the spotlight. The audience began clapping along.

Mrs. Lawson smiled at me from across the stage. She had gathered all my kids to get them ready for their play. Froggy carried the canary cage in both hands.

Our play was about some kids who don't have a clue about how to take care of canaries. I wrote the play with the kids, and I think it's pretty funny.

121

I made my way over to the kids and flashed them a thumbs-up. "You guys are going to be terrific," I said. "Go out there and knock 'em dead."

The jazz band finished to wild applause. I slapped high fives with all the kids as they marched onto the stage.

I felt great. I knew I'd be in trouble at home for sneaking out. But I had to be here to help all my friends.

I felt like my old self again. It made me so happy to know that Slappy couldn't ruin the night.

The curtain opened. The play began. I watched it from the side of the stage. Everyone did an awesome job. The audience was laughing hard.

Froggy almost dropped the canary cage. It was a mistake, but it made the audience laugh even harder.

My heart was pounding. I mouthed every word along with the kids. I was more nervous than they were. But I could see the play was a *huge* hit.

When it was over, the audience roared and jumped to their feet, clapping and cheering. I was so excited, I almost forgot it was my turn to go out and do my act with Slappy.

I hurried to the back wall and lifted the dummy off the floor. It sank limply into my arms. The glassy eyes gazed down at the floor.

"Sorry, Slappy," I muttered. "No tricks for you tonight. For once, *I'm* in charge."

I had plenty of time to think up jokes while I was grounded the past week. And I had a lot of time to practice throwing my voice. Sure, I was a little nervous. But I was also eager to get onstage and make people laugh.

The crowd grew quiet as I sat down on a tall wooden stool at the front of the stage. I perched the dummy on my lap. I stuffed my hand into his back and found the controls for his eyes and mouth.

"Hello, everyone," I said. "I want you to meet my friend Slappy."

Then I changed to my high Slappy voice: *"Get your hand out of my back, Jackson,"* I made him say. *"That hand is cold!"*

"But I have to work your head," I said.

I made Slappy's eyes go wide. *"Oh, yeah? Well, who's working your head?"*

That got a big laugh. I started to feel less nervous. The act was going well.

"No one has to work *my* head," I said. "My head isn't made out of wood!"

"It isn't?" I made Slappy cry. *"Then why do you have termites? Or is that just very big dandruff?"*

"Stop it, Slappy," I said. "Why do you have to be so rude?"

"Because someone is putting words in my mouth!"

That got a big laugh. I could see everyone was enjoying my act. At the side of the stage, all the kids were laughing, too.

"Jackson, do you know the difference between a turkey sandwich and a pile of smelly garbage?"

"No, I don't, Slappy," I said.

"Well, remind me not to send you out to get my lunch!"

More big laughs. This was going much better than I expected. I wished Mom and Dad and Rachel were here to see it.

But, of course, that was impossible. My parents thought I was quietly tucked into my room.

"Slappy, let's do a knock knock joke," I said. I made a fist and tapped his head. "Knock knock."

"Owww," I made him say. *"Knock knock who?"*

"Wood," I said.

"Wood who?"

"Wood you like to hear another one?"

"Would you like me to knock on your head?"

The audience laughed again. This was so much fun. I was having the best time ever.

And then . . .

And then . . .

I heard a loud *chirp*.

34

My breath caught in my throat. I uttered a strangled gasp.

Chirp.

I heard it again.

It came from behind me. To my left. I turned — and I saw what made the sound.

The canaries in the birdcage.

Chirp. Again.

And I began to feel strange. The spotlight dimmed. The whole auditorium darkened to black. The stage felt as if it was tilting beneath me, about to spill me into the audience.

My head suddenly felt heavy.

I knew what was happening. Yes, of course I knew. But there was no way to stop it.

The birds had given the signal. There was no way to stop Slappy from taking over once again.

"This is a great looking audience," he cried. "Great looking if you like a good *horror* show! You all inspire me! You inspire me to *throw up!*"

The audience groaned.

"I didn't say that, everyone," I protested.

The dummy was talking on his own. But who would believe that?

"You know what you all look like?" he shouted. "You look like some warts I had removed! Actually, the warts were nicer looking!"

More groans.

I saw Mrs. Lawson backstage shaking her head and frowning.

"I don't want to insult you people," Slappy said, "but I've pulled better looking *snot* from my nose!"

Silence. I could see the shocked look on some faces. I heard a few boos from the back of the auditorium.

I knew I had to get out of there. I had to stand up and hurry offstage before the dummy caused real trouble.

I tried to jump off the tall stool. But I couldn't move. Slappy was inside my head. He was forcing me to stay there.

"I need help," I called out. "I'm not making him say these things."

People stared at me in silence. *No way* they believed me.

Slappy leaned toward a man in the front row. "Is that your shirt or did you get sick on yourself?"

I struggled to get down. But he held me in place.

I watched helplessly as the dummy brought a volunteer up from the audience. It was a little boy with wavy brown hair and serious, dark eyes.

"Don't stand so close," Slappy told the kid. "Your breath smells like dog poop."

The poor boy didn't know whether to laugh or not. He just stood there gaping at Slappy. I saw that he was trembling a little.

"Don't be afraid," Slappy told him. "I don't bite."

And then Slappy leaned closer to the boy. "Oh, yes, I DO!" he cried.

The poor kid let out a scream as Slappy clamped his wooden jaw onto the boy's wrist. I saw Slappy bite down hard — but I couldn't do anything to stop him.

"Owwwwww! You're *hurting* me!" the kid screamed.

People in the audience started to boo and shout. I saw a few people stomp angrily out of the auditorium. Some people jumped to their feet.

Slappy clamped down harder. The boy screamed.

"Stop! It hurts! It hurts! Make him *stop*!"

I turned and saw Mrs. Lawson striding angrily across the stage toward me. I gave her a helpless shrug.

"Jackson, stop it!" she shouted. "Stop it! Get your dummy off him — this instant!"

I couldn't help myself. I wasn't in control. I couldn't stop.

I leaned forward — and bit down hard on Mrs. Lawson's wrist.

35

She let out a shocked scream. She jerked her arm hard and tried to pull free.

But I clamped my teeth over her wrist.

"Let go of me! Let go! Have you lost your mind?"

She struggled and squirmed. But my teeth were strong. She couldn't get free.

Slappy held on, too. The boy was crying now.

I heard angry voices. Shouts and screams. People were rushing toward the stage.

I knew I was doomed. I would be blamed for everything. No one would ever forgive me for this. And no one would believe the evil dummy caused all the trouble.

What could I do? What?

Suddenly, I knew. At least, I had an idea.

Maybe I could put Slappy back to sleep. Maybe . . .

Maybe if I read those strange words again, they would knock him out.

"Let go of me! I'm warning you, Jackson!" Mrs. Lawson screamed. "You are *really* hurting me!"

Using all my strength, I forced my jaw open.

Mrs. Lawson staggered back as her wrist came free.

I swung away from her. I grabbed Slappy around the waist. His wooden jaw was still clamped tightly on the crying boy's wrist.

I slid my hand up to Slappy's jacket pocket.

Please let that sheet of paper with the secret words be inside the pocket. PLEASE let it still be in there!

I reached into the pocket.

Yes!

The folded-up sheet of paper. It was there! My fingers fumbled around it.

I gave a tug and pulled the paper from the pocket.

Good-bye, Slappy, I thought. *Good-bye and good riddance!*

My hand trembled as I unfolded the paper. I nearly dropped it. But I gripped it tightly and brought it close to my face.

And let out a horrified scream.

36

The paper was blank.

I turned to the other side. Blank. Turned back to the first side. Blank. No words. No secret words. No words at all.

The paper fluttered from my shaking hand.

Slappy finally let go of the kid's wrist. He tossed back his head and opened his mouth in a high, tinny victory laugh.

And what could I do? As everyone stared in shock and horror, I tossed back my head and laughed with him.

That was a few weeks ago. My life has been a mess ever since. I know it will never return to normal.

People stare at me wherever I go. And I hear them whispering about me.

I know what they're saying. They're saying I'm the boy who went nuts and ruined the YC show for everyone.

I'm not allowed to go to the YC anymore. I can

understand why. That little boy and Mrs. Lawson had to have their wrists bandaged.

I feel so bad about that. But I can't explain to anyone what really happened that night.

Mom and Dad have been so worried about me. Of course, I had to be punished for sneaking out of the house. And punished for everything else that happened.

No allowance for the rest of the year. And I'm grounded except for a few school events. No friends allowed to come over. Mom won't even bake my favorite chocolate cake.

I told my parents to throw Slappy out. But they refused. They said he belonged to Grandpa Whitman. "We'll return the dummy next time we visit," Mom said.

So I folded him up and stuffed him into an old suitcase. I carefully latched the suitcase shut. Then I hid it down in the basement behind a pile of cartons.

I felt a lot safer with that evil thing locked away.

But not for long.

One night, I heard voices across the hall in Rachel's room.

I could tell she wasn't on the phone. Who was she talking to?

I crept across the hall. Her door was open just a crack. I couldn't see anything. But I could hear the conversation.

"He was such a good boy," I heard Rachel say. "So totally perfect. Every day, he made me look bad."

Oh, wow. Is she talking about me?

"I understand," another voice said. A voice that sent a shiver down my whole body.

Slappy! She was talking to Slappy!

I pressed my ear to the door.

"I had to show him, didn't I?" Rachel continued. "I had to show him he wasn't so perfect in every way, right?"

"Right," Slappy agreed. And then he giggled.

"So I read those words and brought you to life," Rachel said. "And you know the rest."

They both giggled.

"You've been a good daughter," Slappy told her. "Daughter of Slappy."

My chest hurt. I realized I'd been holding my breath the whole time.

My brain was spinning in my head. Rachel. It was all Rachel's fault. Rachel had been working with Slappy the whole time. She only pretended she didn't know what was going on.

"And you hid those words away?" Slappy asked her.

"Yes. He'll never find them. Don't worry. I hid the secret words and put a blank paper in your pocket."

"Thanks, Daughter."

133

They both giggled again. Then there was a long silence.

Then Rachel said, "Jackson, we know you're out there in the hall. And we know you're listening."

I swallowed hard. My heart skipped a beat.

"And guess what? We know how to deal with eavesdroppers," Slappy rasped.

And then I heard a loud *chirp*.

GOOSEBUMPS MOST WANTED

The list continues with book #3

A BRAND-NEW TAKE ON TERROR!

Goosebumps
MOST WANTED

HOW I MET MY MONSTER
R.L. STINE
SCHOLASTIC

HOW I MET MY MONSTER

Here's a sneak peek!

1

Have you ever felt so frightened, you couldn't breathe? Like your whole body just locked in fear, and you couldn't even blink your eyes?

That's how I feel right now. I can't move and I can't think straight.

My name is Noah Bienstock and I'm twelve. Everyone calls me Bean, even my parents.

I'm underwater. Deep underwater. And it's cold down here. It feels like icicles brushing against my skin. Each ripple of the soupy green water makes me shiver.

I know I have to move. Because something is coming after me. Something dark and big.

I see only a billowing black shadow in the water. Like an ink blot. Moving fast, in a straight line. It starts to take shape. It's some sort of creature.

Ohh. I've seen it before. It's the monster.

I pull my arms forward and try to swim. My muscles don't want to work. The water suddenly feels heavy, as if its pushing down on me, trying to sink me.

The shadow rolls over me, covering me in its darkness, making the water even colder.

I shudder. My whole body prickles from the cold. I want to scream. Scream for help. But I'm deep underwater.

No one can scream underwater. Even in a dream.

Yes, I know I'm dreaming. I've had this dream before.

I know it's a dream but I can't stop my terror. Each time, the dream seems as real as my life. Each time, the monster behind the inky black shadow comes closer . . . closer to swallowing me up.

I ignore my pounding heartbeats and force myself to swim. I kick hard. My hands churn the water. Faster. Harder. But I can't pull myself out of the cold shadow. It reaches over me with tentacles like some kind of octopus.

I can't escape. It's too fast, too big. The shadow spreads over me, making me shudder again as I frantically churn the water. I know the monster is close behind it.

I'm dreaming. I'm dreaming about the monster again. But I can't wake up. I can't raise myself from the green-black ocean depths.

The water bubbles and swirls. Long weeds

slap at my face and wrap around my arms. *Let me go. Let me go.*

My chest is bursting. I need to breathe. I need to scream.

And then I hear a growled whisper, carried by a strong underwater wave. A terrifying low voice, calling to me: *"I'll find you. You can't hide. I promise I'll find you."*

My terror makes my arms stronger. I slap at the water. Push through the long, sharp weeds. Swim up. Yes. My thudding heartbeats are like an engine. I kick and thrash my arms and reach the surface.

Yes!

My head shoots up over the water. I struggle to suck in a deep breath.

But I feel the monster beneath me. I feel it wrap its powerful arms around my legs. And pull me hard . . . pull me down.

I can't kick free. I can't swim. I can't breathe. I can't escape.

Down . . . Down . . .

Wake up! Why can't I WAKE UP?

"I had the dream again," I said.

Mom poured a pile of Wheaties into my bowl. She shook her head and tsk-tsked. "Again?" She tilted the milk carton over the cereal.

"I can pour my own milk," I said. "I'm not a baby."

"I like to pour it," she said. "Makes me feel like a real mom, you know. Like in the TV commercials."

Mom and Dad aren't like TV parents. Mom is a rocket scientist. Really. She's always flying off to some desert to work on a new kind of space rocket. Dad manages a pet shop at the mall. He's always bringing strange birds home to show off to me.

"Why do I have to have nonfat milk?" I grumbled. "It tastes like water. Why can't I have *real* milk?"

She squinted at me. "Because you're a chub?"

"I'm *not* a chub." I slammed my spoon on the

tabletop. "I'm not even the biggest kid in my class. Not even close. Why do you always have to say I'm a chub?"

"Sorry," she said. "Look. Don't take it out on me. Okay? You're upset because of the dream."

"Yeah. Why do I have so many horrible nightmares about being chased by monsters? You're a scientist. Tell me, why do I keep having this underwater dream?"

Mom dropped into the chair across the table and took a long sip of coffee. "Because you're nervous."

"Huh? Nervous about drowning?"

"No, Bean. You're nervous about the swim team tryouts. You're not sure you're good enough to make the team. So you keep having nightmares about swimming."

I stared hard at her. "Maybe you're right."

"Of course I'm right. I'm a scientist."

"But . . . why do the dreams seem so *real?*"

She took another sip of coffee. It must have been really hot. The heat made her glasses steam up. "Because you have a really powerful imagination, I guess."

I liked that answer. I *do* have a good imagination. I think it's because I spend a lot of time by myself thinking up things.

I don't have a ton of friends. I don't talk a lot in school, and it's hard for me to hang out with other kids. I can never think of anything to say.

I think it's because I'm kind of shy. And that makes life a little tough. And a little lonely.

My best friend is Lissa Gardener. She's in my class, and she lives upstairs from me at Sternom House, our apartment building.

Lissa and I look like we come from different planets. I'm short and a little chubby. I have curly black hair and dark eyes and wear glasses like my mom and dad. Lissa is tall and thin, with straight blond hair and blue eyes.

She is trying out for the girls' swim team. But she doesn't have nightmares about it because she knows she's really good at sports. She has other friends, too. But since we live in the same apartment building, we end up spending a lot of time together.

I went to my room and got dressed for school. I expected to find puddles of water on my floor. You know. From my dream.

Bright sunlight filled my bedroom window. But I still saw that terrifying shadow, the shadow of the monster rolling over me deep under the water.

I shivered. I couldn't shake the dream from my mind.

I knew Mom was right. I was just stressed about the swim team tryouts.

I didn't really want to try out. But Lissa said I had to get into some activities at school. She said it would help me make more friends.

I shouted good-bye to Mom. Then I swung my backpack onto my shoulders and headed out the door.

We live on the fourth floor. I never take the elevator. I always go down the stairs. My sneakers clanged on the metal steps as I ran down, my hand sliding down the narrow railing.

I pushed open the door and stepped outside. It was a sunny spring day with puffy white clouds high overhead. The air was warm and smelled of flowers.

I stopped when I saw a red-and-white moving van parked at the curb. A family was watching as movers started to unload their furniture and cartons from the back of the big truck.

A new family moving into the building.

I saw three kids. Two of them were little. But one could be about my age. He turned as I started to walk past. He had brown hair down over his forehead to his eyes. He didn't smile. He turned back to the truck before I could say hi or anything.

Sternom House is very big. Families move in and out of our building all the time. But I always hoped a boy my age would move in, and we could be friends.

I heard a heavy thud as one of the workers dropped a carton off the truck. I didn't wait to see what happened next. I turned the corner and trotted down Elm toward school.

I was halfway down the block, past another apartment house and then a row of little houses. I heard footsteps. Coming on fast.

I didn't have time to turn around. Icy fingers wrapped around the back of my neck.

I screamed. I couldn't help myself. Suddenly, I was back in my dream.

About the Author

R.L. Stine's books are read all over the world. So far, his books have sold more than 300 million copies, making him one of the most popular children's authors in history. Besides Goosebumps, R.L. Stine has written the teen series Fear Street and the funny series Rotten School, as well as the Mostly Ghostly series, The Nightmare Room series, and the two-book thriller *Dangerous Girls*. R.L. Stine lives in New York with his wife, Jane, and Minnie, his King Charles spaniel. You can learn more about him at www.RLStine.com.

The Original Bone-Chilling Series

The Original Bone-Chilling Series